We
Could
Be
Rats

ALSO BY EMILY AUSTIN

FICTION

Interesting Facts about Space
Everyone in This Room Will Someday Be Dead

POETRY

Gay Girl Prayers

We Could Be Rats

EMILY AUSTIN

ATRIA BOOKS

New York   Amsterdam/Antwerp   London   Toronto   Sydney   New Delhi

An Imprint of Simon & Schuster, LLC
1230 Avenue of the Americas
New York, NY 10020

First Atria Books hardcover edition January 2025

For information about special discounts for bulk purchases, please contact Simon & Schuster Special Sales at 1-866-506-1949 or business@simonandschuster.com.

The Simon & Schuster Speakers Bureau can bring authors to your live event. For more information or to book an event, contact the Simon & Schuster Speakers Bureau at 1-866-248-3049 or visit our website at www.simonspeakers.com.

Interior design by Erika R. Genova

Manufactured in the United States of America

1   3   5   7   9   10   8   6   4   2

Library of Congress Cataloging-in-Publication Data

Names: Austin, Emily (Emily R.), author.
Title: We could be rats / By Emily Austin.
Description: [Hardcover edition]. | New York : Atria Books, 2025. Identifiers: LCCN 2024009600 | ISBN 9781668058145 (hardcover) | ISBN 9781668058152 (paperback) | ISBN 9781668058169 (ebook)
Subjects: LCGFT: Novels. Classification: LCC PR9199.4.A92595 W4 2025 | DDC 813/.6--dc23/eng/20240304
LC record available at https://lccn.loc.gov/2024009600

ISBN 978-1-6680-5814-5
ISBN 978-1-6680-5816-9 (ebook)

For my rat sisters
Mallory and Ainsley

Author's Note

This book deals with suicide, and it does so through the perspective of a person who treats their death, at first, as trivial.

Suicide is never trivial. If you or anyone you know is struggling, help is available.

For support in the USA and Canada, call or text 988.

Sigrid's
Note

Attempt One

Sorry. I tried to pick a date that would be least inconvenient for you. I was tempted to do this in December, but I drew Jerry's name for Secret Santa, and I couldn't stomach the idea of everyone unwrapping their gifts while Jerry got squat.

It's always a pain when people try to squeeze things in over the holidays, so I held out. I appreciate that this is annoying, no matter the season, and hope you won't let it ruin your Groundhog Day. I don't know if a note will make it any better. I figured I should write one just in case it might. I'll leave it up to you to decide. If you think this will make it worse, burn it. Pretend I never wrote it. Tear it into pieces and flush it down a toilet.

If you decide to read this, please keep in mind it's my first suicide note, and I'm a bad writer.

By the time you kick the bucket you're supposed to have wisdom to impart, but I don't have any. Most people die more experienced or well-read. I did read this book once where a rat goes on a veritable smorgasbord at a fair. He feasts on candy apple cores, salted almonds, and rejected hot dogs. He's a gluttonous rascal, so he has the time of his life, wolfing down trash until his belly distends and he becomes a fat rat ball.

I'm not sure I'd recommend taking the advice of an uneducated, twenty-year-old dead woman, but if you insist, I might say you should try being like a rat at a fair. To be clear, I don't mean that you should gorge yourself on carnival garbage. I just think you should try to collect days like that. Do whatever will turn you into a rat ball, so to speak.

This one night, when I was a fourteen-year-old rat ball, I ran around town with Greta. We slurped blue raspberry slushies and snapped firecrackers at squirrels. I know now that was animal abuse. To balance out the image of squirrel cruelty, I want you to know it was a picturesque summer evening. There were fireflies in the grass. It wasn't too hot or too cool, so I wore shorts with a windbreaker. I could hear crickets playing violins, and the sky was bubble-gum pink. The streetlights had just turned on. We darted beneath them like they were spotlights and we were stars on a stage. My skin felt hot but not burnt from the day, and the air smelled like bug spray and charred firecrackers. Greta's laugh was catching. It was the kind of laugh that made everyone else laugh, even if they missed the joke.

I was giving the squirrels voices. We would spot one and in a squeaky voice I'd say, *"Spare me, girls, please. I have a family."*

Greta laughed so hard I felt myself float, happy as a rat with a hot dog. At the time, I had no idea how few days like that we get.

When you're a kid, you assume you're just getting a taste for all the memorable experiences life has in store for you, but the truth is, most people don't spend countless nights running through the streets with their friends. They spend a handful of nights doing that if they're lucky.

Greta and I used to spend a lot of time scavenging for change to buy corner-store slushies, cannonballing into the creek, and swinging in parks past sundown. There are only so many days in a year, and a lifetime. There aren't enough carefree days like the ones I had with Greta, I guess. I think of those times as scarce and precious now. I didn't appreciate them then. I do today. Now I'd say traipsing around town with Greta is as close as I got to eating carnival trash.

If you're still reading, I don't want a funeral. I would hate to think of anyone taking time off work just to attend. Margit would have to drive in from out of town. I would rather you didn't bother. Unless, of course, you would like the excuse to get together.

You should check if you get days off for funerals that you wouldn't get off otherwise. If that's the case, you should pretend you're throwing me a funeral and just take the day. Go to the movies or something. Have a picnic.

Try not to treat my death like it's some big miserable catastrophe. There is a dark lens to suicide, and in most cases, there *should* be. It's devastating to picture someone so hopeless they would rather die than go on. The sister of a kid at my high school killed herself, and I remember roaming the halls like a zombie after the news broke. Students were sobbing into the shoulders of teary-eyed teachers. It was traumatic. In this case, though, there's no need for heartbreak. I understand it's unpleasant to face death, especially self-imposed death, so I don't want to invalidate your feelings. But it's a bit complicated why it had to be this way, and I don't want to get into the hairy details. Trust me, this isn't a tragedy.

To be honest, I'm not sure I fully grasp the meaning of the word "tragedy." My English teacher gave us a whole mind-numbing lesson on it once. We were studying *Hamlet*. She droned on and on for forty minutes about tragic flaws and Julius Caesar. Is it Julius? Or is it Juliet? I don't know. I wasn't paying attention. I was too busy carving my initials into my desk and tearing pages out of my notebook to fold into those little paper fortune teller games. When I did listen, I was confused. Shakespeare confused me. I think it's pure gibberish.

My point is, while I understand there is an inescapable dreariness to death, mine is a whole different can of worms. Or a different kettle of fish. Or whatever the correct idiom is. Is "idiom" the right word?

How long are these things usually? How am I doing so far? I hope you get what you need out of it. If you threw this out, that's okay. I don't mind. I'm dead. Besides, writing this is a cathartic way for me to kill time before I kill myself.

I'm on my period. I need to wait for it to end before I can free my horses. I don't want to be buried with a tampon in. I don't think that even death could halt my period. I think my uterus would continue to shed for its usual seven long days. Funerals are normally scheduled within the week of death, and I've got it in my head that my mom might try to bury me in a white dress because she never got to witness me make an honest woman of myself. I have this mental image of a blood spot growing across my dress as I lay in an open casket in front of everyone I've ever met. Rather than position my body and memory to suffer that humiliation, I've decided to wait for my period to stop.

Sorry if period talk repulses you. Maybe I shouldn't have included that. I'm not up to speed on suicide note etiquette. I always found etiquette in general difficult to grasp. My sister used to elbow my ribs and say, *"Shh. That is inappropriate."*

All I'm trying to get at is that most of us with young uteruses can't just kill ourselves or go to the beach willy-nilly. We have to consider how our periods impact our suicides. But maybe I'm not supposed to say that. Maybe I'm supposed to come up with some palatable lie as to why I'm waiting to pull the trigger.

Forget what I said about my period. Let's say I'm killing time before I kill myself because I have big plans this weekend. I'm going to a pool party. I'm hoping to get a suntan.

I don't know if I've hit the mark with this note yet. I'm worried my death might bum you out, so I want to leave you with something to cheer you up. Is it working? How are you feeling? Good?

I guess my goal for this might be a little ambitious, given the context. I have a history of overestimating myself. I used to think I could do anything. I thought I could break world records. I could be famous. I could go to the moon. That mindset trickled down into everything I did. I'd heap more food on my plate than I could eat. I'd tell myself I could walk distances I couldn't. I always ended up scraping excess mashed potatoes into Tupperware and collapsing in the dirt, miles out of town, with wobbly knees. Maybe I'm doing something similar here. Maybe I'm setting myself up to fail, thinking I can write an upbeat suicide note.

Picture that I wrote this naked. Would that make it funny?

No. That would probably make it unsettling, right?

Picture that I wrote it drunk.

No. That would be disturbing too, right?

Picture that I wrote this with a happy heart, sipping an iced coffee, eating a donut. That's the truth. I've got a Boston cream clamped between my front teeth right now. I'm eating it hands-free as I type. I'm scooping vanilla custard out of the fried dough with my tongue. I feel happy.

I want you to feel similarly. I don't want to upset you with this. I hate being the source of anyone's distress. I wish I knew exactly what to write to cheer you up. I was never fully in tune with how the things I said and did would be received by others. Sometimes I spoke, intending to make things better, but accidently made them worse. Once, for example, I tried to comfort Margit after she got dumped. I said, "Good riddance, that guy looked like a deep-sea fish."

What I was trying to communicate is that she could do better; however, she did *not* receive that message. Instead, she cried, "That's the most insensitive thing you could have said to me. You're telling me that even a guy who looks like a blobfish can't love me?"

That made me laugh because I hadn't specified that he looked like a *blobfish*—I said "a deep-sea fish"—but she knew which fish I was thinking of because he looked just like one. I couldn't help but find that hysterical. I was in tears. She wouldn't speak to me for a week.

Picture a blue sky. Imagine you hear mourning doves cooing, a breeze gusting through tree branches, and someone far away laughing. Pretend you see sunlight glistening in some babbling water, you smell fresh-peeled oranges, and there's, like, a Great Dane puppy panting beside you, or something.

Sorry. I'm not great at influencing people. I'm trying to make you feel good. I'm probably not supposed to say how I want you to feel. You're not supposed to know what my objective in writing this is.

I'm just supposed to slyly meet the objective. I'm supposed to make you feel sunny and comforted without telling you explicitly, "I want you to feel sunny and comforted when you read this." I wish I were a better writer.

I wasn't born with that skill people like Margit have, where they're so keyed into everyone that they're capable of guiding how others feel. She senses how what she says will be received by others. She's capable of de-escalating tension, distracting people, avoiding touchy subjects, and wording herself delicately. I'm not. I never say the right thing. I think Margit absorbed all of that skill in the womb and left me deficient.

Is what I'm saying right now upsetting you?

I wonder, Margit, if you get your hands on this before other people do, could you please edit it for me? You're a better writer than I am. I want this to be the kind of note that gives people closure and consoles them. I don't want it to bum anyone out.

You wrote almost every essay I submitted in high school, and you're an English major now. I stopped handing in my homework after you moved out for college. Maybe that's why I didn't graduate and made so many spelling mistakes. Have I made any in this note?

Marg, if you have the time to spare between Shakespeare and your Postcolonial Literature class, could you please take a scalpel to this? Erase parts. Change my wording. Fix my spelling. Take liberties, okay?

Regarding the squirrel story, I was trying to describe a time I felt genuinely happy. I wanted to paint you a goodbye portrait of me, sun-kissed, laughing. I wish that memory didn't involve tormenting squirrels. I wish Greta and I had spent that evening picking wild-flowers or something. We didn't though. We painted penis graffiti on the underpass by our high school, egged a teacher's house, and lobbed firecrackers at squirrels. To be clear, we didn't kill the squirrels. We just put the fear of God in them. I guess it is possible one scurried off to perish in a tree hole somewhere. Being spooked can kill little creatures. They have tiny, pea-sized hearts.

It would be a better memory had the squirrel part been omitted. It would be inauthentic not to mention that, however, and I don't want to lie to you. That would ruin this, right? My intention is to lift your spirits, and people don't like to be lied to. If I told you some sanitized memory that made me look good, and you found out parts were fabricated, you might start wondering if I lied about being happy at all that night, right?

Do you lie a lot, Margit? Is that how you influence people? You nod along and agree to comments you don't actually agree with? You pretend you're not upset when you are?

Maybe my problem is I'm too honest. I want to be honest, though. Smacking squirrels was the principal part of that evening. I wish it weren't, but that's the truth. I felt happy spray-painting penises on an underpass and frightening harmless animals once.

Maybe I should workshop a different happy memory entirely. That was just the first one that occurred to me, but I have others. I have loads.

Attempt Two

The first high school party I attended was in the woods. I was invited by a senior football player while in line at the school cafeteria. I went despite noticing he and his friends were only inviting girls from the ninth grade. I considered that creepy and off-putting, but not enough to forgo my first high school party. When I arrived, I was relieved to see older girls there, too. One of them told me the football team invited ninth-grade girls because they had already dated everyone else. I watched those guys approach girls my age as if I were watching feral hogs in rut. It felt both disgusting and depressing to witness a pack of drunk boars pester piglets.

There was a bonfire. They strung fairy lights from the trees and tapped a keg. I remember inhaling the smell of burnt pine needles and watching the sky turn orange through the trees. I gawked up at the branches, like a canopy above us, and imagined they were long, knobbly monster fingers grasping at the moon.

I always imagined fanciful things like that when I was a kid. It was a trick I used to make life more stimulating. When I bit into fruit, for example, I pretended I had never eaten fruit before. I imagined fruit only existed in fairy tales, and that by some miracle I'd found a wild orchard. I would rip the barcode sticker off an apple, press my nose against its skin, inhale, and bite as if I were crunching into something enchanted.

I imagined roads were oceans. The floor was lava. Grass was dyed coconut shavings, and the earth was a giant macaroon. There was this cornfield near my house I used to cut through. When I was in that field, I imagined I was one inch tall. I pretended the cornstalks were blades of grass, and I was a gnome trudging through a lawn on my way to my home in a hollowed-out mushroom.

I was thirteen at that party. Around that age, I had begun imagining things less. I found myself eating fruit and walking through cornfields, thinking, *I am eating fruit*, and *I am walking through a cornfield*. Before I fell asleep, I used to fantasize about things like bathing in chocolate rivers and having a pet unicorn, but at thirteen I found myself ruminating about conversations I'd had. I thought about changing my hairstyle, and about what happens when you die. My thoughts were rarely about garden gnomes, unicorns, and other little girl things anymore. I was a teenager, and it was getting worse.

I remember feeling this sharp ache in my calves. It was severe enough that it woke me up at night. What was that? Was I feeling my bones grow? Or my muscles stretching? Or was it something else? Every morning I woke up sensing I'd grown overnight. I didn't just feel taller, I felt like I was digesting my child-self and morphing into someone new.

Before caterpillars become butterflies, they turn into guck in their cocoons. They don't just grow wings from their caterpillar worm-bodies; their old body breaks down into a liquid, and their new body forms from the remains. I felt like I was guck, and my body was a cocoon. I felt like I was absorbing myself, becoming a whole new bug, and I didn't want to be. I preferred to be a worm. I liked my worm-thoughts. My worm-body. I didn't want to change.

I wasn't the type of kid who wanted to be a teenager. I wanted to be a kid. I felt sort of trapped inside my new adolescent form, and worried about how torturous the rest of my life would be, jailed in a grown-up's body. I grieved for my toys, and for the person I was the year prior. I felt like I was dying and being reborn as someone dead-me couldn't stand.

It was September. The temperature had cooled. I had just started high school. Greta and I had homeroom together. We had spoken a little in class. I stood beside her at the firepit, listening to the crackle of the flames, watching sparks glide through the air and burn out at our feet. The wind kept shifting, so we moved together to avoid the smoke. Our eyes were watering. Neither of us were talking, so after a while I nudged her arm. I pointed at the branches above us and said, "Those are monster fingers."

She looked up and squinted. "Oh yeah, I can see that too."

We sipped our drinks and shifted again with the smoke. She gestured down at the roots weaving in and out of the dirt beneath us. She said, "Those are tentacles."

I smiled. Music was playing. People were shouting. I waved at the air. "They're casting spells."

She held her beer up. "This is a witch's brew."

We were both grinning. She and I clicked.

I was anxious about making new friends when I started high school. Most teenagers seemed to be on a different page than me. They wanted to be more grown-up. I felt out of place. I worried I'd have to pretend that I was someone else to fit in. I'd have to play that I was interested in dating senior football players. I went to that party thinking I needed to act more like the people my age. But then I met Greta. Within moments of speaking, my worries subsided, and I knew I could be myself.

After drinking three beers under the monster fingers, I confided in her that I hated being a teenager. I said I wished I could be eleven years old forever. She agreed. She said she felt the same way. She told me her friends were all excited to be in high school, but she wasn't. She hated it.

We commiserated about how predatory boys in the twelfth grade preyed on our friends that night. We griped about how everyone was changing; they were all morphing into pubescent monsters who had forsaken their Barbies and cartoons to discuss blow jobs and go shopping. We both felt out of place and strange.

During that conversation, I was convinced I'd found the one person on earth like me. Greta ranted about her friend who got a new boyfriend and no longer had the time of day for anyone else. I watched her talking as if she were my favorite Barbie come to life. The bonfire cast this flickering light on her face. She complained that her friend had become a shell of her former self. Everyone was becoming a shell of their former selves. She felt like she was a shell.

My friends and I had drifted apart too. When we were kids, we bonded over our shared interests in pretending we were all witches, and in making up imaginary pet dogs. During middle school, that changed. Every conversation was about which boy they had a crush on, diets, and TV shows I didn't watch. I found myself listening quietly to conversations, picturing our imaginary dogs lying lonely in a corner, all our magic draining from our feet.

Greta and I spoke fervently at that party. Despite looking nothing alike, we stared into each other's faces as if we were mirrors of each other. At one point, we clasped each other's hands.

In retrospect, I bet a lot of kids feel troubled when their friends change. I'm sure it's common to feel distressed when you mature, stop daydreaming, and begin spending too much time considering the shape of your bones. Still, no one was saying that to me besides Greta. Everyone I knew seemed keen to digest themselves and forget their worm-bodies. There was something special about finding someone during a time when I felt like I was losing everyone.

That night, she and I chugged beer like it was potion. I forgot all about my bones. I roared in the woods like an animal. She and I climbed a tree. We threw a dried-up, dead bush into the fire. We listened to the sparks crack, and I screamed that I could hear God. A boy drove me, Greta, and a gaggle of girls from the woods to get gyros. We popped our heads out of his sunroof and grinned into the night air like we were dogs on a car ride. The radio played a song everyone knew the lyrics to. We belted out the words, and I felt alive. I watched my weary hometown blur by and felt strangely charmed by it. I started hating Drysdale sober, and dreamed of moving away.

I had these visions of myself on the moon, in a big city, or in the ocean. I wanted to migrate, like animals do, to an environment better suited to my nature. I wanted to live near something exciting— like shooting stars, jellyfish, or mountains. I wanted to look out my window and see something more interesting than potholes or dads mowing their lawns. I wanted to live among animals, or with aliens, or at least around people who had bigger things to do than spray pesticides in their gardens, go to church, and complain.

That night, the streetlights looked brighter than usual, and the houses all looked like they were made for Victorian dolls. I thought maybe Drysdale wasn't so bad. I considered for the first time that being a teenager might be fun. I remember looking at Greta and believing that I saw her completely. I felt like I had tapped into some magic power that allowed me the ability to see people fully. I felt awestruck by her. I recognized in her face that she had suffered, and that she was important. I knew she looked at me the same way, and that we expressed our deeply felt connection by laughing and shrieking into the ether.

I woke up the next morning barfing, hating myself and my hometown again, but I felt fortified with the knowledge that at least I wasn't alone.

———————

That story derailed. I remember feeling happy that night, but binge drinking, barfing, and hating yourself isn't exactly better than abusing squirrels, is it? Be that as it may, it stands out as one of my happiest memories. I had to include the dark bits because what made that memory bright was how stark it felt in the pit of being a thirteen-year-old girl.

Let me try again.

Attempt Three

My grandma took me to Walmart once when I was eight. She needed to buy shoes. While we were making our way to the back of the store, I spotted a doll on a shelf with the laundry detergent. She was a Barbie with long chestnut hair, a purple backpack, and miniature silver binoculars. I'm sure she originated from a toy aisle with rows of dolls identical to her, but on the detergent shelf she stood out like a fat ruby. I thought she was one of a kind.

When I first spotted her, the store went quiet. It felt like all the fluorescent lights dimmed except for the one above her. She had cobalt eyes with little white sparkles dotted in her pupils. I thought I saw the sparkles materialize the moment she and I spotted each other.

While Grandma tried on orthopedics, I gazed adoringly into the doll's face and named her Jo. She was strapped in her box behind a sheet of plastic. Her little wrists and ankles were cuffed in twist ties.

I rubbed my own wrists while I looked at her. I was eager to free her from her container. I lugged her around the store while my grandma examined her feet in those little ankle-high mirrors.

Boxes of shoes accumulated next to Grandma while I whispered to Jo about our basement. I had erected a civilization for my toys down there. The basement wasn't finished or anything. It was an empty room with a water heater, a furnace, and a cracked concrete floor. The walls were covered in pink fiberglass insulation that I was always tempted to touch. My dad must have noticed my interest. He warned me whenever he was tinkering in the basement. He said, *"You know not to touch the walls down here, right?"* The basement smelled musty, and there was a constant hum from the furnace.

I shared a bedroom with Margit. She didn't like to play the way I did, so I spent most of my time alone beneath the house, constructing a miniature world for my toys. Marg once stuffed a pillow under her shirt, declared she was with child, and said a bad guy was after us. She told me we needed to hide to protect her unborn baby. I remember crawling under her bed while she whispered to me to be quiet. She said, *"Try not to breathe."* I didn't like playing with her. I didn't want to hold my breath, feel scared, or pretend Margit was grown enough to be a mother. I preferred to imagine we had magic powers. I wanted to pretend we were happy lizards, eating bugs, or something.

Margit stopped playing with dolls way before I did. My bed was crowded with stuffed animals for years, while hers was bare. She took up reading. She bought makeup. She got into boy bands. She was only one year older than me, but I felt like she was elderly, and I had just been born. Adults used to tell us that one day we'd be close, but that never happened. There were times when I thought I hated her. If we weren't sisters, we probably wouldn't have been friends. Though maybe it's harder to be friends with someone who you shared a bedroom and parents with. Maybe if we had met as adults, things would have been different.

At eight, I thought of our dank basement as paradise. I built dollhouses out of what others thought of as garbage. I used flowerpots, egg cartons, and shoeboxes. I looked through our recycling bins regularly, pulling out anything that could be transformed into something for my toys. I made tissue-box beds, and bottle-cap stepping stones. Every inch of the basement was covered in mini streets and neighborhoods. I pretended that the insulation in the walls was cotton candy, and that my toys lived in a utopia where the clouds were made of Barbie-pink spun sugar.

I told Jo about my toys at home. Most of them came from thrift shops or were hand-me-downs from people my parents knew. I had a name, a history, and a thorough biography for every toy I owned. I collected Barbies, troll dolls, stuffed animals, Polly Pockets, Playmobil, and other little plastic animals and dolls. I told Jo that there was a Lego bridge currently under construction, and a new community garden—which was the corner of the basement where real clover sprouted through the crack in the floor. I described the cotton-candy clouds.

After my grandma finally selected her new shoes, we approached the cash register. I asked her in my purest voice if we could please buy Jo. She replied no, and my heart sank. I thought I heard Jo gasp too.

I was the type of kid who believed that toys had hearts and souls. I felt like I was ditching a new friend, abandoning Jo in that Walmart. I begged Grandma to reconsider, like I was begging her to allow someone who was drowning into our lifeboat. She said, *"No, you have so many dolls already,"* so I left Jo on a rack with magazines, covered my face with my hands, and cried.

About a month later, on my ninth birthday, Grandma gave me a yellow gift bag. I pulled the white tissue paper out, spotted Jo's sparkling eyes, and sobbed. I clarified that she was the Jo I met; she wasn't a different version of the same Barbie. My grandma laughed. *"Yes, I bought her the day you asked for her. I snuck her to the cashier with my trainers.*" She was smiling wider than I had ever seen her smile. The happiness I felt radiated from my nine-year-old body and seeped right into Grandma's.

———————————

My grandma is dead. That memory might not be uplifting because it features two deceased people. That might be depressing. Would you prefer a memory with living people instead?

Attempt Four

One night, Margit and I skated on that frozen stormwater pond in the center of our neighborhood. The sky was dark, but the snow reflected the moonlight, so I could see Margit's face like it was midafternoon. Her cheeks were rosy, and she had snowflakes caught in her eyelashes.

Margit and I butted heads a lot growing up. When we were kids, I was hyper and loud. She was quieter and more reserved. We irritated each other. Most of my sisterly memories were tainted by fights we had. When I thought of our parents driving us anywhere, I saw Margit and I in the back seat, arms crossed, huffing. When I thought of our sleepovers at our aunt Jerry's, I saw us kicking bruises into each other's shins on her pull-out couch. I had scars on my hands where Marg bit me, and I remember ripping out fistfuls of her silky hair.

That night, we didn't fight. We looked up at the flurries weaving down from the heavens and tried to catch snowflakes on our tongues. We held each other's mittened hands and spun in circles until our lungs burned from the cold. I remember running home, pretending that the snow on the ground was icing. We played that we were two little candlesticks slipping on an icy cake. We shrieked "*Happy birthday!*" as we skidded down the road, imagining our winter hats were candlewicks on fire.

Maybe that's a better memory than the other two. Did you prefer it? I felt a sort of run-of-the-mill kind of happiness that night, but maybe that's the superior type. A lot of my memories of my sister— even my happy memories—are complicated, but there were also plenty of times, like that night, when things were simple.

Whenever I visualize snow, I always think of that metaphor about how no two snowflakes are the same. That was nailed really hard into me when I was a kid. When I examined snowflakes up close, I wondered whether I was unique too. I walked around all winter thinking I was one of a kind. I thought it that night when I saw the snow caught in Marg's eyelashes.

I'm not sure why we tell kids everyone's so unique. We aren't really. I get wanting to make kids feel special, but most people are more of the same. It might be easier to grow up if kids weren't sold this tall tale that we're all exceptional. It might make it less jarring to become an adult if we knew the truth the whole time. We're mostly ordinary.

Do you think of this kind of thing when you think of snow? Do stories containing snowflakes make you feel dull and average now too?

I'm trying to write positive memories to make you feel good, but I keep missing the mark. Something murky always snakes its way in.

Nothing is ever purely good, in any case, is it? That's just the truth of it. There is a rotten piece to everything. Whenever you pick up something comely in the wilderness, like a good-looking twig or a nice rock, worms are always exposed, wriggling in the dirt.

All I'm trying to get at is that I have felt enormously happy. I cackled around town, drank myself gay, loved a doll, and watched snow plummet from the sky. I can't imagine anyone has felt happiness more profoundly than me. I got to the peak. I don't intend to kill myself because I'm unhappy. This has nothing to do with that.

Attempt Five

Are you in the right headspace to read this? There are a few practical things I'd like to address now, but before diving in I just want to check in with you. Are you okay?

My primary intention for this note is to cheer you up; however, it's inescapable that suicide notes read a bit grim. Every attempt at this I've made so far has felt heavier than I intended. Part of the complication is that I *am* in the right headspace. I can see the upside to this; however, I can also appreciate that others might not feel as optimistic as me, the suicidal person.

I want you to know that I didn't do this because I was depressed. I'm not depressed. In fact, I feel great. Don't get me wrong, my life isn't perfect. I didn't graduate high school. I live in a basement. I worked thanklessly at the Dollar Pal, and I keep getting into arguments with my family. I can see how you might spin that to argue I died of misery. I really didn't, though.

Things were going well. I was making my own money. I had my own place. I spent most of my spare time doing things I enjoyed, like smoking weed and watching *Jeopardy*. When my head hit my pillow at night, I drifted off happily. In fact, if I suffered from an imbalance, I might argue I had a disproportionate helping of the cheery chemicals.

I'm not the same person my family knew when I was a kid. I think some of you might picture me that way—when I was little, playing with Polly Pockets, missing baby teeth. Or do you picture me as a teenager? A reckless, immature person who thought she was invincible? I wasn't really either of those people anymore. I changed, or was changing, at least.

Shortly after I moved out, I stopped by the house to visit. Mom had just made Millionaire Chicken Casserole. I don't know why she called it that. It had crushed Ritz crackers sprinkled on top. I doubt rich people eat that kind of delicacy. I liked it when I was a kid, but I'd become a vegetarian since I moved out.

Mom offered me a plate. I said, "Thank you, but I don't eat chicken anymore."

She exhaled as if I'd just cussed her out.

Margit was visiting too. She said, "Just eat around the chicken."

I said, "That part still has chicken residue in it, and I'm not hungry anyway."

Everyone rolled their eyes as if I wasn't eating the casserole solely to piss them off. Dad said I was exhausting. Mom said, "What kind of person doesn't eat chicken?" Margit tried to change the subject. She started talking about the novel she was reading.

I got up and left. As I was opening the door, Mom shouted that I was dramatic.

I stopped coming by. I rarely answered the phone or called. I kept you all at arm's length. I found it hard to get along with you. Even when I tried, we argued. I always left our interactions with my heart rate up. Because of the distance between us, I felt like you didn't really know me anymore. Did *you* feel like you knew me in the last couple of years?

I wasn't a difficult person around other people. In fact, I don't think anyone outside of our family would describe me as exhausting or dramatic. I think you might have a warped perception of me. People saw me differently than you saw me. I saw myself differently than you saw me.

I was someone who went to trivia on Tuesday nights with friends I made at work. I knew most of the answers to questions about geography and pop culture. The people there said I was smart, which was new for me. I don't think I've ever been described as "smart" before.

My boss told me I'd make a good manager because I was personable, organized, and quick. He always asked me to train new hires. Don't get me wrong, I wasn't the best employee to ever grace the Dollar Pal, but I wasn't a total slacker, and my manager thought highly of me.

I was dating someone. She and I broke up recently, but on good terms. I met her family. She told me they said I was charming. She may have just been pumping my tires, but still.

I kept a journal. I knew how to make leek and potato soup. I paid my bills on time. I did my laundry every Sunday. I owned a mop, and I kept my apartment clean.

Does any of this surprise you?

I think you thought of me as someone who didn't have it together. I think I was our family's scapegoat, or something. I was a distraction from the real underlying issues in our dynamic. I think I bore the brunt of the negative attention. I was compared to Margit, who was responsible, earned good grades, and was off making something of herself. I didn't finish school, I had undefined goals, and practiced what Mom referred to as "an alternative lifestyle." I think, for Mom and Dad, a girl who has it together is someone on course to meet societal expectations. She's on track to have a good job, a house in a nice neighborhood, a husband, and babies. I certainly wasn't on that track.

Despite all of that, I think I did have it together. Maybe I didn't have *everything* together, but I wasn't totally lost. I wasn't completely off course. I wasn't childish. I wasn't totally irresponsible, or difficult to get along with. I know that I'm partly responsible for the tension between us. I'm not trying to paint myself as some holy saint who was victimized by you. I had issues—I just don't think I had as many as you thought I did.

Everyone was so disappointed in me when I didn't graduate high school. You were all so proud of Margit for going to college. She was the first person in our family to go. You seemed to think of me as some lost, stunted kid who made bad decisions and needed to smarten up.

And I probably did need to smarten up. I know I made some bad decisions. I was disappointed in myself for not being more accomplished too, but I don't think I was as senseless as you thought I was. I was doing okay. I was happy.

I am sad that I won't get to witness Mom, Dad, and Jerry finally retire, or Margit graduate. There are things I would have liked to see, like the northern lights, or beluga whales. I'm disappointed to die before discovering who wins the *Jeopardy* Tournament of Champions this year, or to find out who gets elected mayor. There were also some mysteries I'd have liked the answers to. Not the big ones; I don't care whether aliens exist, or what the deal is with God, but I had some smaller-scale questions.

For example, someone was shoplifting googly eyes from the Dollar Pal. I found myself replenishing the googly eyes every time stock came in; however, I never once sold a pack. It concerned me, not because I took issue with shoplifting, but because I didn't understand why someone would steal so many googly eyes. Who was taking them? What were they doing with them? Why?

I also would have liked to know who was making those bomb threats to the building next to the Dollar Pal. I was evacuated almost weekly for the last four months. Cops would barge in and scream, *"Vacate! We got a bomb threat!"* The first time it happened, I dropped everything. I even left the cash register unlocked. But it started happening so frequently, it lost all novelty. They were obviously prank threats. When the police came in shrieking, I'd say, *"Yeah, yeah,"* finish ringing up my customer, and leisurely lock the register. I started thinking, *Nice, I get an impromptu day off.*

I don't know why anyone would threaten that building. It's not a particularly hostile building. It has a dentist office in it; it's where adult ed is, and some municipal government offices. I don't know why anyone would want to intimidate a dentist, adults trying to get their high school diplomas, or small-town public servants, but I guess we all die with some questions unanswered. Maybe if I died elderly, or even middle-aged, I'd have more wisdom about that. Maybe there's some grand purpose to having unanswered questions. Maybe I'd be more at peace with it. Who knows?

Despite feeling a little sad to miss out on the future, and to die wondering what causes rainbow lights in northern skies, I still feel content with my life. Overall, I feel good about it.

How about you? How are you feeling? Are you sad because I'm dead? Would it help to hear a joke?

Why didn't the skeleton go to the party?

Because they had no body to go with.

I'm sorry I couldn't think of a funnier joke.

Because their heart wasn't in it?

Because they didn't have the guts?

Speaking of hearts and guts, if it's not too much of a hassle, one thing I would like to address now is organ donation. I was not taking exceptional care of my body, but if you could try to salvage anything functional, that would be much appreciated.

I'm sorry if this is too much information, but I was having sex with a woman before I died. I know that is a prickly subject for some of you. It's an example of something my sister might nudge my ribs about. I need to be forthright because I think there might be some weird AIDS hysteria surrounding that and organ donation. They might not accept my organs. That might only apply to gay men, but I'm not sure.

If it were up to me, I would lie to the organ donation people. I would tell them I was straight. It seems a shame to waste a pile of perfectly good, life-saving organs, doesn't it? It is terrible to think of someone dying due to my squandered pancreas. I'll let you decide for yourselves. I'm not going to force your hand into pretending I haven't been having sex with women. I have been, and if you are not comfortable pretending otherwise, and the donation people don't want my organs, that's fine.

Maybe you could donate what's left of me to science. I think that might mean scientists will handle my naked body, which is a shame, but that's okay. If you get wind that someone I once knew has become a scientist and might run into my cadaver, could you please ask them to request someone else's? It is no big deal if you can't, but if it's easy.

I heard about this guy who donated his wife's body to science. She was blown up in missile testing. He was distraught. He didn't feel like that was the best use of her. He wanted her to be used to cure a degenerative disease, or something.

I don't mind if they use me for missile testing. In fact, maybe suggest it—that way we can spare folks like that guy from having their wife's body blasted.

Is this getting too morbid? It's tough to avoid being morbid in a suicide note. I'm sorry if I'm making you feel uncomfortable. Marg, maybe you should erase this. What do you think? Does it matter more that I express my will and testament in terms of donating my organs, or that I don't make people feel icky?

I have you listed as my next of kin, Marg. Maybe you could handle this whole organ job privately and erase this part of the note? If you can't figure out a way to donate me, that's okay. Don't worry about it.

Either way, I don't recommend telling Jerry that I wanted to be donated to science. She doesn't trust scientists. She thinks they planted the dinosaur bones. She thinks most fossils are fake, and that vaccines are part of some pedophilic agenda to kill old people. I can't bear to imagine what she would think scientists want with my corpse.

I would prefer no funeral, but if you would like one, please tell everyone to wear yellow. Better yet, treat it like a Halloween party. Come dressed as peacocks or corpse brides. Tell everyone they can't wear black unless it's part of their costume.

Please dispose of my phone and my computer without looking at their contents. I did my best to erase what I could, but I was not as technologically savvy as I would have liked. I would prefer to die knowing someone better apt will sort that all out. I don't want to find myself rolling around in my grave while you discover how frequently I googled "Dame Helen Mirren Bikini," or any of the other humbling aspects of my search history.

Please also dispose of my diary. I considered burning it myself, but I live in a basement apartment, and I didn't want to accidentally murder the people who live above me. I also didn't want to get fined by the fire department for burning it out on the lawn.

———————

When I was sixteen, I burned my school notes in my parents' backyard. I was celebrating the summer holiday. It was a small fire. It didn't last long. Nevertheless, we got a warning from the city. They sent an ambulance, two cop cars, and a fire truck. I was treated like an arsonist for lighting up a couple of shabby notebooks. The sirens inconvenienced the neighbors.

My parents were incensed. Any time they found a lighter in my pocket from then on, they thought I'd been out starting fires again. Meanwhile, I was just innocently making apple pipes and smoking weed in people's garages.

I found it strange that Drysdale devoted so many resources to one sixteen-year-old burning her homework, and so little to some of our bigger issues, like the opioid epidemic, homelessness, and rampant hate crimes, but I guess that's none of my business.

If you're asked to identify my body, you might need to know about a few tattoos you're probably unaware of. If you see them, and question whether the body is really mine, it is. I've been wearing clothing that hides them. I'm sorry you had to find out this way, though I suspect the criticisms I would have received are moot now. (*You will never get a good job . . . You are going to look weird when you're old . . .* , etc.)

I have a great white shark tattooed to my chest, a piece of Lego tattooed to my foot, a skull on my shoulder, and Revelations 17:5 KJV on my back. That's the biblical passage that says, "MYSTERY, BABYLON THE GREAT, THE MOTHER OF HARLOTS AND ABOMINATIONS OF THE EARTH." I got that one with Greta. She got it on her shin. It's a friendship tattoo.

———————

Consider not telling old people I died. I don't think they need to know. Just pretend I can't come to events, give them generic updates about my life, and spare them the news. Realistically, I only see those people once every couple of years, and they only have a few years left in them. Why trouble them? Let's approach this the same way we have approached my sexual orientation. I think they could die none the wiser, don't you?

I googled the cost of caskets, and it's criminal. Please bury me in a garbage bag. I have also discovered that tombstones, which are just slabs of rock, cost thousands. Please consider laying a patio stone where you bury me. They make patio stones that say things like GRANDMA'S GARDEN and LOVE GROWS HERE. I think they could make one with my name on it. Maybe you could get them to write something funny. I bet asking tombstone makers to carve jokes on stones is more uncomfortable than asking someone to produce a novelty garden rock. Get them to write BURIED ALIVE or HELP! on mine. That might be funny. Or you could skip the stone entirely. It feels like a needless cost, doesn't it? Though it is worth considering that there's a practical benefit to having a marker where a body is buried.

My grandma dug up part of her garden one summer when Marg and I were kids. She wanted to grow rhubarb, or zucchini, or something. Sadly, while digging, she uncovered the remains of a big dog. I remember seeing its skull. Grandma was an avid Great Dane owner, she always had one. The gruesome discovery just about brought her to her knees. A family had lived in the house before her, so the remains must have been of their old pet. It would have been nice for her to have been given some warning, via a tombstone. I imagine that scenario would play out even more grimly with human remains, though my grandma really loved Great Danes.

I feel bad leaving everyone with my death's expenses. I wish I had saved up for this. I didn't know it was so pricey. If you can't find an affordable approach to my death, just drop me at the dump, okay? Toss me in a landfill.

This is getting too morbid again, isn't it? Do you think I'm being insensitive and gruesome? That isn't my intention. I'm trying to do what Marg always suggested I do, which is be polite. I know you won't really throw me out at the dump. Offering that suggestion was my roundabout way of communicating that anything you do is generous.

If I wrote, frankly, *anything you do is generous*, you might suspect me of being self-serving. You might think I was just trying to appear kindhearted. It's rude to try to appear kindhearted, right? The polite thing to do is to communicate that *anything you do is generous*, without implying that I am wonderful for saying so. The only way that I can think to do that is to establish that I'm horrible, by writing things like, *bury me in a garbage bag*. Do you get it?

I never really honed being well-mannered, did I? My instinct is to be direct, but that's often rude. For example, you can't say, *I want to go now* when you want to go; you have to say, *Well, I've had a lovely time, but sadly I'm beat*, even when you are an insomniac, or you've had espresso, or done coke, and know you're going to be up for hours. Sometimes I think I accidentally made up white lies that were ruder than telling the truth.

I'm sorry if this is rude, but I'm going to be direct now. I feel terrible for killing myself. I really do. I had to do it, given my circumstances, but it's not lost on me what a burden this is. I wish there were some other way. I know you're all very busy, and that you have enough on your plates without having to deal with the costs and logistics of my untimely death.

To be even more direct, I know that the cost and logistics of this aren't the biggest burdens I'm leaving you with. It's awful when someone dies. When Grandma died, I felt torn in two. It's probably worse in this case because I'm young, and I doubt anyone expected this. The least I can do now is assure you that you should buy the cheapest death supplies you can find for me. Get me the plot in the graveyard next to the bathrooms or in the corner where they bury the murderers—

Sorry, I'm doing it again.

Attempt Six

I hope that girlfriend I recently broke up with doesn't read this. Actually, she wasn't really my girlfriend. We didn't put a label on it. She's left town, but there's a chance she might come back knocking on my door. If she finds out I died, she'll be pissed. She said, *"Creeps like us have to stay alive."* She always talked about how important it is for there to be creeps roaming the earth. I don't know why she thought I was a creep. I think her definition of "creep" might be different from mine.

If you run into a twentysomething girl with purple hair and a tattoo of a black cat on her shoulder, wandering around town searching for a creep—don't tell her I died. Say I was abducted by aliens, or something. Say I joined some counterculture, anarchist community. She'd be into that.

I deactivated all my social media accounts and would like to ask that no one create any content on the web regarding me. Please do not name any charities after me. Don't share a photo of me on my birthday or my death day. While I appreciate the sentiment, I don't want that kind of attention. I would prefer to die a quiet death.

Remember when Mom tried to throw me a birthday party last year, and I refused to come? And everyone was mad at me? And Jerry posted that huge block of text on the internet about how Mom put all that work into the event, and I didn't show up because I have issues? I'm sorry about that. I wanted to come, but Jerry was right. I did have issues.

I would like to address Jerry, Marg, and everyone else who replied to Jerry's post last year. I imagine you might feel a bit remorseful now that I'm dead. You posted negative comments on the internet about a person who killed themself. I'm sorry for putting you in that position. I will be honest and admit that a small part of me feels vindicated because there were about a dozen harsh comments under that post, calling me rude. I feel like everyone who commented lost sight of the fact that despite it being true that I was rude, it was nonetheless my birthday.

Despite all of that, I would like to acknowledge and forgive you. Please don't beat yourselves up about it.

I wonder if anyone is actually going to read this. Did you throw this out? Has this been flushed down a toilet? Am I writing to myself?

Hello, Margit?

How are you?

I'm good. I got an unexpected day off work due to another bomb threat. I hope if anyone is reading, they're feeling good too. Do you think they are feeling sad because I'm dead?

Probably a little, yes. It's always sad when people die. Hopefully they're not too sad, though.

Are you too sad, possible reader? How is your headspace? If it's bad, you should try to get your adrenaline pumping. Try introducing yourself to a stranger, taking a cold shower, singing karaoke, or telling someone a secret. Dopamine is harder to voluntarily produce than adrenaline, and they are similar hormones.

If that doesn't work, maybe go pour yourself a glass of water, eat some cruciferous vegetables, take a nap, and try to get some vitamin D. I've also heard that omega-3 fatty acids and magnesium are beneficial for mood. It might help to take a walk. Try that and come back. I don't want killjoys dampening the mood of my death note.

Are you wondering why someone like me, a suicidal person who has assured you that I am not depressed, knew so much about dopamine and omega-3 fatty acids? While I recognize that might seem suspicious, given the context, I promise I really am not depressed. The girl I was dating was, though. She saw a therapist, took Zoloft and everything. In addition to those forms of treatment, she also did things like eat fortified cereals and exercise. She said that helped her. When that didn't work, and she felt especially low, she would do things that scared her.

Her dad died right before we met. She was going through a tough time. She behaved a bit manically. She wanted to do dangerous things. We often spent our time together climbing on the roofs of tall buildings at night, driving over the speed limit, and doing Ecstasy and weird sex stuff. I'll spare you the details of the weird sex stuff. While I would get a posthumous kick out of my suicide note being a

detailed account of the spooky sex I was having before I died, I have
an inkling that might put my family off.

Are you mad at me? It's okay if you are. Is my tone making you
madder? I bet it is. I bet you're furious. Your cheeks are getting so
red. Turn around! I'm standing right behind you!

Made you look. I'm not really standing behind you. I'm dead.
And again, I'm sorry if you're pissed at me about that. Or about my
tone. I recognize that despite wishing this could be treated as trivial,
there is gravity to it. I get that, I do. In normal circumstances, I
would classify suicide as tragic. I just think that we should approach
my particular death a little more gaily, and as the victim of this, I
would like to ask that you extend me that courtesy.

Now, you might be thinking that I am also the perpetrator of
this, and while that's fair, I didn't have much of a choice. I don't want
to get into all of that. That is not the point of this. The point of this
is to tell you all goodbye and good luck. I want each of you to know
that I had no hard feelings toward you. I wish you well, and I don't
plan to haunt any of you. Not even you, Jerry.

Attempt Seven

*E*rase everything I've written so far, Marg. The tone was off, and it was all over the place. I wasn't accomplishing what I set out to do. Please consider that rough work. Consider it trash.

I'm trying again. This time will be better because I've warmed myself up. I'm going to make this attempt more formal. I think that will improve it. When you write too informally, it reads psycho-pathic. I want this attempt to be more official. I want people to read this and think, *Wow, she really knew what she was doing.*

Dear family, friends, and colleagues,

It is with utmost regret that I must inform you I have passed away. The circumstances surrounding my death are complicated, but technically—in terms of what the coroner will classify this as—it was suicide. I apologize for the disquiet you might feel given the circumstances, and for all the hassle.

I want to assure you that, while I am sad I won't see you again in this life, I'm not dying due to sadness. This isn't that kind of suicide. I had terminal brain cancer. Rather than succumb to that, I chose to die peacefully with pain pills, or something. I am still working that part out. All to say, please don't worry about me.

Regards,
Sigrid

How was that? Is it too formal now? Did you find it stiff? I should change "Regards" to "Love," right? Suicide notes probably warrant a "Love" closing. I don't know who is going to read this, though. There are a few people I don't love who might. If that girl I was seeing read it, for example, it might freak her out. We were only dating for like four months. What if my coworkers read it? I don't want to sign off "Love" to the people who work at the Dollar Pal. That's unprofessional.

Should I mention the cancer? I feel weird about that. Mostly because I don't really have cancer. I just wrote that I did in that letter because I thought it would make things cleaner and easier to explain. It's sort of like when Mom said we couldn't go to Disney World as kids because Disney was closed, when really it was because we couldn't afford it. It was just easier to say it was closed than to explain socioeconomics to children.

I'm sorry for treating you like children. I'm just trying to make this easier. I don't think it serves anyone to get into the real details, but if you really want to know, I had this terrible pain in my chest. It affected my breathing. I went to the emergency room. I got a CT scan, an MRI, and an ultrasound. It turns out, there was swelling in the blood vessel that carries blood from my heart to the rest of my body. I had a thoracic aortic aneurysm. It could have ruptured at any minute. It was like living with a ticking bomb in my chest.

Doctors were monitoring it, and I was given this medicine, but it wasn't working. It was a very large aneurysm. I was lined up for surgery, but the thing was huge. I had to sign a waiver that said my chances of dying during the operation were high. I didn't have it in me to go through all that. Do you understand? I wasn't built to be this brave person who could withstand that kind of turmoil. I wasn't the right person for the job. I'm also of the belief that dying feels better than worrying you might die at any minute. Do you know what I mean?

I should have started drafting this earlier. I'm a real procrastinator. I knew I was doing this. I planned to do it in January, but I realized that was too close to my mom's birthday. You can't kill yourself near your mom's birthday. It's insensitive. Then it was getting too close to the city's election, so I stuck around to vote early last week.

That last draft was too cold, I think. I need to find the right balance between being casual and stiff. I need this to be the suicide note equivalent of pairing a blazer with jeans and a graphic tee. It needs to be business casual.

Or maybe I should try to make it sound more flowery. What do you think? Maybe I should make it the equivalent of a statement dress, or yellow overalls, or something. Maybe it should read more like a poem. That might be good, right?

Dearest world,

Forgive me for my early send-off. I love you to the sky and back.

Meet me in the clouds.

Eternally,
Sigrid

How's that? It's terrible, isn't it? If someone killed themself and left me a half-assed fluffy note like that, I'd be livid. I would rather they leave nothing than that. It's insulting.

Should I write separate notes for different people? That seems like a lot of work, but maybe it's warranted. I'm not sure what the procedure is here. There's no one I can ask. I'm nervous if I google it, cops will show up at my apartment.

I bet the cops are way too busy to monitor my internet usage. They have homeless people to kick out of vestibules. That one Black man who occasionally drives through town isn't going to pull himself over. It's probably more likely that Drysdale police spend their time gossiping with each other in parking lots or texting their mistresses—though Marg would nudge me for saying that.

Attempt Eight

Dear Mom and Dad,

I'd hoped I would be an easier kid for you as an adult. I know I was a handful growing up, and that you were worried about me. Remember that time I got caught shoplifting pens? Or all the times you thought I was out starting fires? I wish I could stick around and stop causing you grief, but the universe works in mysterious ways, I guess.

I promise I wouldn't have done this if I didn't have to. My intention wasn't to upset you. I'm grateful to you both for everything, and I really am sorry about this.

I'm sure you're both mad at me. I bet you would prefer I try to save myself, or let nature run its course. You want me to avoid committing a mortal sin; however, we all know I already committed quite a few mortal sins, right? I just mentioned

*shoplifting, for one. There were a few others we didn't discuss
as openly, but I think it was obvious I already had a pretty
stacked pile.*

*All to say, I'm not concerned about adding another sin to
my pile. Furthermore, and with all due respect, I would invite
anyone opposed to my mortal sinning to take a quick peep
in the mirror. Suicide is a sensationalized mortal sin. I don't
know a single soul who isn't guilty of at least one of the less
theatrical ones. Did you know extreme anger and despair are
mortal sins?*

Anyway, I hope you can forgive me, even if God can't.

Here are my dying wishes for you:

> *Be nicer to each other.*
>
> *Don't vote for Kevin Fliner to be mayor.*

I'll meet you in heaven.

> *Love,*
> *Sigrid*

Attempt Nine

Dear Jerry,

Thank you for being there for Margit and me growing up. You were like a second mom to us. I want you to know that, even though we argued a lot in the last year or so, I really appreciated you.

I remember when you would take us shopping. You let us get things Mom wouldn't. I got to buy clothes from the boys' section, and Marg got to buy underwear that didn't come in a ziplock bag. I remember you picking us up from school when we were sick, when Mom and Dad were working. You and Mom always joked about how when I was a baby, I'd run to you when I was hurt instead of her.

I don't understand why you're voting for Kevin Fliner. The man doesn't support recycling programs, Jerry. He wants to do

*away with compost, and that's the least of it. He doesn't believe
in climate change or evolution. He thinks our library should be
defunded until they ban gay books, and he wants to hire a police
chief who's been accused by three women of domestic assault.
He thinks the opioid epidemic can be stopped by closing the safe
injection site downtown. I've struggled to reconcile how you could
support someone who is so openly odious that it's almost absurd.
He's like a comic book villain; he is the caricature of a bad guy.
Do you not see that?*

*I was having a tough time with you before I died. Sometimes,
I worried I hated you. I want you to know now I didn't. While
I found your recent political and social behavior morally
abhorrent, I loved you. I died thinking of you sticking Band-Aids
to my baby knees. I know that you contained multitudes.*

*There is something I'd like to get off my chest while I have
you. I'm the reason your Facebook got suspended. I reported
your posts for misinformation and hate speech. You were always
posting about essential oils being better than modern medicine,
as well as thinly veiled transphobic, sexist, and racist memes.
I'm not sorry I did that, but I am sorry for letting you think the
government was censoring you.*

My dying wishes for you are:

   Stop eating essential oils.

   Don't vote for Kevin Fliner.

   *Listen to people who have different experiences
      than you do.*

*Love,
Sigrid*

Attempt Ten

Dear Marg,

I'm sorry we fought at Christmas. I wish we hadn't. When we were kids, everyone always told us it was normal for sisters to bicker, and that one day we'd become best friends. That never happened, though, did it? If anything, we drifted further apart in the last couple years.

I want to explain my point of view at Christmas. I wasn't able to communicate this very well to you at the time because I was flustered. I had a lot going on.

The reason I got angry at Mom was because she kept using the R-word. I wanted to correct her. I wanted to explain why that word shouldn't even be in her vocabulary. Every time I opened my mouth, she said it again. I ended up putting my fist into a pie and flinging pastry and cherry filling across the table at her *because I was rattled by my outrage, and by my inability to form words.*

You looked at me like I was possessed. When I watched the red goo drip down Mom's frock, I wondered it too. When I stood up from the table, I didn't feel angry. I felt insane. I left the house amid the thunder of everyone yelling that I was nuts.

You followed me outside and told me I ruined everyone's Christmas. I told you to fuck off. I pretended I was leaving because I had irritable bowel syndrome and felt sick. You said I was being an asshole. You said I needed to think of others more. I needed to be more sensitive. I remember looking at the pie filling under my fingernails while you told me to grit my teeth more— like you do.

I was always gritting my teeth, Marg. I had TMJ from clenching my jaw so hard. My jaw clicked every time I yawned. I cared about upsetting people. I knew I shouldn't have thrown pie at Mom. I knew I should have handled that differently. I cared about ruining everyone's Christmas. I didn't throw pie at Mom because I wanted to wreck her day.

I threw pie at Mom because I lost control of myself. When I was in that house, it was like I reverted back to being a kid. I felt immature, under attack, and crazy. I thought of my child-self, sitting cross-legged in the basement, holding a doll, listening to our parents scream at each other while you hummed that everything would be fine. I thought of what I'd do now as an adult if I came upon that scene; if I saw two little girls in that house with parents behaving like jackasses, and I snapped. That's why I didn't go there often. Every slight, everything that offended me, hit like a major blow. I was carrying a bag of grievances. I knew that even the slightest addition could break me. I felt like a shaken bottle of Coke, dodging the Mentos everyone was trying to toss inside me, already liable to explode. I needed to escape.

I wish you and I hadn't fought. I wish I hadn't thrown pie at Mom. I wish we lived in a utopia where the sky was made of pink cotton candy and there was never any conflict.

You and I used to escape together. Do you remember being shipped to Jerry's when our parents were fighting? Jerry had that ratty old love seat that pulled out. You and I always slept on it, with the bar in our backs, and no space to roll over. Despite that discomfort, and the secondhand smoke that clung to everything at Jerry's, I always felt content to be at her place, didn't you? Remember how she always fed us Froot Loops and Wonder Bread with raspberry jam in the mornings? She gave us complete control over her TV.

Remember that time, after Jerry went to bed, and you and I watched late-night sex line commercials? We were both aghast. Our Catholic school education had tricked us into thinking everyone was chaste until properly conjugal. We watched women posturing in lingerie for hours, the realization that we'd been duped washing over us.

The next morning, you and I both woke up exhausted. We had stayed up late with the ladies on TV. Remember how I approached Jerry about what we'd seen? I said, "Jerry, be honest, do people have sex before they're married?"

You elbowed my ribs, and Jerry was taken aback by the question, but she said, "Yes, honey. They do." *That was a revelation, wasn't it? You and I gawked at each other like the time we unearthed where our tooth fairy money came from. You choked on your Froot Loops, and I hushed the word* "fuck" *for the first time in front of an adult.*

When we were old enough to notice that we were sent to Jerry's every time our parents' arguments escalated to a boiling point, I asked Jerry if she thought they would ever get divorced. She said, "No, don't worry, girls. They're Catholic."

I know you don't like it when I talk about our parents fighting throughout our childhood. You prefer to reminisce about Grandma's garden, or the old cartoons we liked to watch. I was willing to talk to you about daylilies and Rugrats, *but any time I broached the topic of our parents' misconduct, you as good as put your fingers in your ears. It felt like I couldn't talk to you at all anymore. After you moved out, there was this massive divide that grew between us. Did you feel it too? I wish we talked more. It's probably rude of me to bring this up now when you can't elbow my ribs or shush me.*

The problem is, I think one of the benefits of growing up with a sibling is having a witness. It's nice to have someone to cross-reference your childhood with. I feel guilty leaving you alone. I wish I could stay to corroborate your memories. I promise not to dwell on this, but since I have you, if I have you, I want to share a few things. You can skip this if it bothers you. You can erase it if you'd like. I am going to write it out, just in case you're open to reading.

Did you know it's abnormal to be able to identify a person by their footsteps? Or by how they open doors? We were too aware of the sounds in our house because we were on edge. Our parents were volatile. We had to pay attention to whether Mom and Dad were slamming doors or stomping down the stairs. We were tuned in to their behavior, listening for warning signs that their tempers were rising. We were living in that house like frightened rabbits, twitching our ears to the sounds around us like prey in constant danger. Did you recognize how my steps sounded? I knew you by yours. I'd know it was you walking with my eyes closed. Do you still walk like a mouse on her toes? I know every family has its hitches, and that sometimes you just have to grit your teeth, but I think maybe we're supposed to examine what's wrong, or

*it festers. This is me doing that, okay? This is my attempt at
facing those problems.*

*Do you remember how we used to pretend a monster lived
in our house? We said he had giant swamp-man feet, fangs, and
hair like a lion's mane. I always pictured he was green and scaly.
I imagined tentacles growing out of his head. We pretended when
we heard shouting or something break, the swamp-man had
woken up.*

*Obviously, the swamp-man wasn't real. He was just Dad
when he was angry. Sometimes, he was Mom. You and I
generously decided that when they were in good moods, they
were our parents, and when they weren't, they weren't themselves.*

*Now we know the truth is that they were always themselves.
They weren't complete swamp-monsters, and they weren't
completely good. I'm not writing this now to attack them. I
know it might read that way because this is my suicide note
and acknowledging your parents' faults in your death note reads
harsh, like blame. That is not my intention. I'm just trying
to be honest. I was not completely good, or a swamp-monster,
either. There is just a rotten bit to everything, and to everyone,
right?*

*Remember that time Dad punched a hole in our bedroom
wall? He was angry that he couldn't find the remote. He thought
one of us had lost it. He thought maybe we had even hidden it
from him. I remember you and I shrinking beneath him while he
loomed over us like a snake over raw baby birds. In my memory,
his skin was green.*

*Once, before we went to bed, you told me what an empath
was. You said you thought you might be one because you always
had such a good grasp on what other people were thinking. I
agreed with you at the time, but now I'm not so sure. I think
you just read the room, monitored facial expressions, and*

*tried to anticipate how other people were feeling, because our
parents couldn't control their emotions. You were on guard and
tuned in to people out of self-preservation, because our parents
behaved like temperamental dogs. Dad would explode at the
drop of a hat, and you could never predict how Mom would
react when you asked for a favor. Sometimes it was, "Yes,
of course," and other times it was, "How dare you? You're
ungrateful."*

*I know things could have been worse and that nobody is
perfect. I know they worked hard to take care of us. I know they
both had difficult childhoods. If I had kids when I was eighteen,
I would have fucked them up too. If I had a dog, I would have
fucked it up. I would have fucked up a gerbil.*

*You always said you were introverted, but I don't know. You
might just get tired carrying the mental load required to monitor
everyone around you. You seem to spend every interaction
scrutinizing every glance, every move, every word, every laugh.
You seem compelled to help ease everyone's mounting feelings; to
distract people, to redirect conversations, to explain what someone
meant when you notice a misinterpretation. You were always
shushing me. Elbowing my ribs. I think it was because you
watched Dad for signs of his temper rising. You paid attention to
how hard Mom shut the cupboards, to assess her mood. It looked
exhausting.*

*My approach to our parents' tempers was to disengage, while
yours was to dial in excessively. If our parents were a TV show, I
was in the next room, chasing a butterfly, tuning out. You were
pressed up against the screen, your hair static, your eyes wide and
glued to the glass. Ultimately, I don't think either approach was
healthy. I think you're neurotic and controlling because of it, and
I was detached and delusional.*

*I used to think I could do anything. I thought if someone
attacked me, I would muster superpower strength. I thought*

if I set my mind to it, I could be a millionaire. I could be an Olympian if I had any interest. I could be a doctor, a pilot, a zookeeper. I could start a farm or breed Great Danes. I could shape-shift. I could become a shark if I mobilized the will. I could fly. I didn't think those last, more magical goals, would be easily achieved, but I did believe that if I rallied every ounce of my will—I could do anything. I really thought I was invincible. I did things like run across crumbling train bridges at night. I rode in the backs of pickup trucks driven by plastered teenagers with bongs clinched between their thighs. I let a high stranger do a stick-and-poke tattoo on my foot in her basement. Rather than feel like a powerless baby bird, I chose to believe, despite all the evidence to the contrary, that I was invulnerable and capable of anything.

You saw us as flightless baby birds, didn't you? You knew we were vulnerable. That's why you were always on defense. You were trying to protect us. You were reserved, self-conscious, and careful. You nodded along when Mom, Dad, and Jerry did ignorant things, because you wanted to avoid conflict. You almost always behaved. You did well in school. You flew under the radar so you could escape, so everything could be tolerable. You found me frustrating because I wasn't like you. I rolled my eyes when Jerry talked about essential oils. I had outbursts. I threw pie at Mom. I yelled that Dad was deranged after he punched a hole in the wall, and you cried at me to shut up. I didn't have the same restraint you had, and I cared less about avoiding conflict than I did about speaking my mind. You were so high-strung, anxious, and mad at me all the time. I found it hard to be around you.

You and I were affected differently, and obviously I'm no psychiatrist, but I think the root causes of our issues are the same. I don't want to be negative. I want this note to be uplifting, but I

think ultimately it is uplifting to acknowledge this. I'm dead, and
you could probably live your whole life exhausted, nudging people
in the ribs, making up swamp-monsters, but I wouldn't choose
that for you.

Love you,
Sigrid

Attempt Eleven

Dear Greta,

I don't know what to say.

Attempt Twelve

Scratch the personal letters. I think they're over-the-top. I regret writing anything negative. In fact, I'm going to write some nice things about everyone now, to negate mentioning all that swamp-monster stuff.

Every time there was a bomb threat near the Dollar Pal, I got a text from my dad. He listens to a police scanner while he putters around in the garage.

He'd write me,

Are you okay?

Dad's not much of a texter. I've witnessed him attempt to type on his phone, and it's like watching a hooved animal try to play a string instrument. I knew that every time he wrote me, Are you okay?, it took him fifteen minutes.

If I didn't reply, he'd call me. When there was a bomb threat, I usually left with that girl I was seeing. I rarely looked at my phone when I was with her. I wanted to disconnect from my real life and be who I was with her.

I have a bunch of messages on my voicemail that he accidentally left by not hanging up fast enough. In one of them, I can hear him muttering to himself, unaware he's recording.

"I hope she's okay."

Once, a raccoon broke into our house. It was my fault. I left a basement window open. He skulked inside overnight and pillaged my toy civilization. I went downstairs after school, and it looked like a tornado hit. All my little fences and trees were knocked over. Toys were scattered everywhere. I didn't notice the raccoon at first. I froze near the bottom step, trying to remember if Margit and I had fought the night before. I worried maybe she had gone downstairs and enacted some revenge.

When I first spotted the raccoon, I thought he was a stuffed animal. I knew all my stuffed animals, so he stood out. I thought maybe he was Margit's. Maybe she had accidently left him down there after plundering my city.

I didn't realize he was a real raccoon even when he moved, because everything moved for me in the basement. I had a lively imagination. The dolls' mouths opened and closed when they spoke. The tinker cars drove up and down the streets. The miniature plastic dogs rolled in the grass. There was wind.

I screamed when I saw him, not because I realized he was a living wild creature, but because he was holding my doll Jo under his armpit. He was carrying her like he was King Kong. Even while

I screamed, I didn't know he was real. I thought he was just a mean stuffed animal. I thought he was some villainous toy who had broken into my utopia to attack Jo and fuck shit up.

My mom rushed to the basement. She said, *"What happened? Are you hurt?"*

I pointed at the raccoon.

With zero hesitation, she ran to get our hamper off the dryer. She stormed downstairs, grabbed Jo from the raccoon's armpit as if he were a shoplifter, threw the hamper over him, and sat on top of it. The raccoon scratched at the basket like a prisoner clanking a tin cup against jail bars.

My dad arrived home shortly after the raccoon had been trapped, and he and my mom figured out a way to release him outside. I remember them shouting at each other the way football players do, as if getting the raccoon out of the house was a tactical play in a game. After he was released, he scuttled across our lawn like a freed hostage. I remember him looking back at us over his shoulder.

After he was gone, my parents came back down to the basement. They helped me prop my toy fences and trees back up. Marg came downstairs to help, too. Jerry and Grandma stopped by later, and they also joined the cleanup. Together we sanitized my plastic toys and tossed my stuffed animals through a gentle cycle in the wash. Everyone helped me put my little world back together.

When it was nearing Margit's prom, my mom took us to a dress shop. The plan was for Margit to try on some dresses, and for Mom to make her one based on which she'd liked best. We didn't have money to buy prom dresses. Our family was outfitted by Walmart and secondhand stores. I remember wearing out the soles of my off-brand sneakers. There were holes in the heels. My shoes were always full of pebbles.

Margit stood on a little podium in front of a mirror and tried on what felt like a hundred dresses. I didn't really want to be there. I didn't care about dresses; however, Mom said she would take us to Cinnabon after, and I had been bribed places for less.

When Margit was a teenager and she tried on clothes, she rarely asked if they looked good on her. Instead she asked, *"Do I look normal?"* She always looked normal to me, but I guess her standard was different from mine. She wanted to blend in completely. She didn't want to be different at all. Often, in our bedroom, she would make me look at her outfits before leaving the house. I knew my job wasn't to tell her if she looked nice. It was to tell her if she had camouflaged her weight well enough. She would ask, *"Should I add a cardigan?"*

If it were hot out, and I said, *"No, it's hot out,"* she would glare and ask again, suggesting the question wasn't really whether she should add a cardigan. It was, *Do I look fat?*

She looked miserable trying on prom dresses. Most of them didn't fit. The dress employees clipped them to show how they would look in her size. Her skin was flushed. It wasn't just her face, but the skin on her back and her upper arms. She looked red and uncomfortable. Despite that, a lot of the dresses looked good on her. I knew I couldn't say that because she thought they looked bad. She would have snapped at me as if I were making fun of her. So I sat silently and thought of Cinnabon.

That is, until one dress. It was embroidered tulle, I think. I don't know fabrics well. It had sheer sleeves, a sort of corset, and little dainty flowers stitched into it. It not only fit her, but it really suited her. She looked at herself wearing it in the mirror, the red in her skin cooled, and you could tell that she knew she looked pretty.

My mom asked how much the dress was. It was expensive, so Margit took it off. She tried on a few other dresses that didn't compare, and then we left to get Cinnabon. Marg didn't eat any of her cinnamon bun, while I licked the icing off the cardboard box mine came in, and Mom yammered on and on about how she was sorry we couldn't afford that dress. She said she would try to make it.

A few days later, when Marg and I got home from school, the dress was hanging up in our room. Spotting it felt like that moment in Cinderella, after her dress is ripped apart by her stepsisters and she opens her armoire to find that pretty gown stitched for her by friendly mice and birds.

Mom and Dad had gone and bought the dress. They probably maxed out a credit card or sold something. I was behind Margit when she opened the door to our room and first spotted it. She gasped, *"My dress!"*

On the day of Marg's prom, I noticed Mom had tears in her eyes when Margit came out of our bedroom wearing the dress. Dad snapped a picture of her, and he never takes pictures. Last I saw, his phone had two photos in it. Margit in her prom dress, and a screenshot of some wrench he wanted to buy.

I didn't go to my prom. They had a rule that you had to be graduating to go. I was failing English. I was told I'd be permitted to attend if I handed in my final English essay, but I didn't.

I liked going to school dances when I was a kid. That changed when I got to high school. Dances started putting less emphasis on music and fun, and more on outfits and dates. I felt out of place. The only thing worse than wearing a formal dress in my mind was not wearing one and being a dressless spectacle. If I had gone wearing some gown, everyone would have commented, *"Oh my God, you're in a dress!"* and if I hadn't, everyone would call me a lesbian (derogatorily).

Additionally, the thought of my parents making or buying me a dress felt sad. Especially when I considered Margit's prom the year prior. I would have felt obligated to try to fool everyone into believing I loved a dress the way Marg did.

Greta didn't go to prom either. She also didn't feel comfortable wearing dresses. She and I spent our prom night sitting on an electric box behind the mall, smoking weed. We bought Chinese food from the food court.

There are a lot of events in life that are romanticized in movies, books, and TV, like prom. The actual experience is never really what's promised, is it? I remember being in middle school thinking that high school was going to be this whirlwind where everyone was dramatic and fun. I pictured crowds of teenagers laughing in school hallways, pep rallies, school rivalries, love triangles, and food fights. I thought I'd care more about our football team. Maybe I'd join a clique. I'd have this cinematic, teenaged experience. I'd hark back on my time there when I was an old lady, as if they were the golden years of my life. The reality of high school wasn't anything like that. Though maybe that's because I wasn't the teenager I was told I would be. Maybe for some people, events like prom feel the way they're supposed to.

Not going to prom made Greta and me feel like we were missing out on something; however, we knew we would miss out even if we went. We were sort of fated to miss prom, regardless of whether we attended. She and I used to talk about how a lot of life felt like that, like we were never the target audience for any of it, like we were always on the outside of something.

The truth is, theoretically, we wanted to go to prom. Theoretically, in a world where going to prom wouldn't entail our clothing being a spectacle, where everyone didn't comment on whether we had dates or we didn't, we would have gone. If the evening wasn't bogged down with all of that—we would have liked to go. We probably wanted to go as much as anyone else did. Maybe even more. If the world worked for us the way it seemed to work for other people, we would have had fun at prom. We loved parties and being places with crowds of other people. We loved feeling like we were a part of something.

Despite the complicated sentiments I had about prom, I had fun that night with Greta. I remember watching her struggle to spark a joint and laughing. It was windy. We were high, eating chicken balls and chow mein, getting sweet-and-sour sauce caught in our hair.

If I hadn't met Greta, I think I would have gone to prom. I think I would have worn a dress I felt uncomfortable in. I would have found some guy to escort me. Sometimes, I think if I hadn't met Greta, my whole life would have felt like going to prom—like I was in a costume I hated, but on the outside, secretly pretending to feel what everyone else does.

Because I had Greta, and she had me, we realized we had the option not to go. Instead, she and I got high and walked around Drysdale, cackling like we were the town's witches. We ambled all the way across town, stood in that cornfield on the edge of the city limits, looked up into the night sky, and pretended we were gnomes.

I felt comfortable being myself around Greta. Sometimes, when I was around other people, I pretended to like the TV shows, celebrities, and music they liked. I laughed at jokes I didn't really find funny. I tried to be someone I wasn't. I felt like a bird in a monkey costume, standing in a crowd of real monkeys, hoping no one would notice my feathers.

Finding Greta felt like clocking another bird in a monkey costume. She and I were alike. We could talk to each other about worms and building nests, while the monkeys discussed bananas, and debated how many of them would need to press on typewriters until one of them wrote *Hamlet*.

She and I were comfortable being ourselves around each other. I felt as at ease in her company as I did when I was alone. With other people, I felt an awkward divide. Even in large groups, that distance made me feel lonely. In a lot of ways, I didn't relate to other girls my age. For example, I couldn't understand why so many of them liked Max Holmwood—a serial cheater, who seemingly bathed in Axe cologne and called girls "broads." It made me feel insane. I often wasn't interested in what they were interested in—like Max, other boys, fashion, makeup artistry, and other feminine hobbies I was unfamiliar with. It's not that I thought badly of those things (besides Max), I just didn't understand. Likewise, they didn't seem interested in what I was interested in, like Cate Blanchett movies or felt-frog miniatures. We had a different lens on the world. They were monkeys. I was a bird.

Greta and I had the same lens. We understood each other. We both exchanged bewildered looks whenever a new girl confessed that she had a crush on Max. We wore boyish clothes and no makeup. We had no interest in talking about fashion or futures motivated by becoming wives to husbands or having lives that were anything like our parents'. We had similar tastes and interests.

I told her things I couldn't tell other people. There were parts of myself I hid around others. I kept a diary. I felt insecure. I worried I might be stupid. I told her I thought I couldn't do well in school without Margit's help. I told her about my family; how my parents got into violent arguments, how we had money problems, and how Marg and I fought. I confided in her about everything, and she did the same with me. I knew all about her family, her parents' divorce, her secrets, aspirations, and insecurities. She and I trusted each other.

She always assured me I wasn't stupid. She told me she believed I could do whatever I wanted. I felt the same way about her. I think we gave each other confidence. It's occurred to me that everyone needs someone who understands them and believes in them. Having even one person who really gets you, and likes you, feels sort of vital for survival. Greta and I were that for each other, I think. We were real best friends.

I wonder who will read this. I doubt any of my friends will. None of them are big readers, and most of them have moved away for college, had babies, developed opioid addictions, or transformed into grown-up strangers. The people I go to trivia with aren't close-enough friends to read a suicide note. Greta and I don't speak anymore.

Before dying, I mostly hung out with that girl I was seeing. I didn't confide in her much. We spent our time together doing things like pool hopping and talking about politics and the news. Occasionally she opened up to me about her problems, but I rarely told her mine. Most of this letter would probably read to her like a stranger wrote it.

I wonder if my parents or Jerry will read this. I have a feeling they might not. It's hard to tell with them. I think they'll be mad I did this. They might refuse to read the note. Maybe, after a few years pass, if this is left somewhere they can read it without anyone knowing, they might.

Who am I writing this for? Am I just writing this for myself?

Remember our bunk beds, Marg? I wanted the top, but you got it because you're older. I remember putting my legs up between the slats above me and kicking your mattress. You would shriek at me to stop, but I wouldn't. Sometimes I'd pretend to stop and start again when you didn't suspect it. You'd roar above me like I was poking a literal bear.

You usually prayed out loud before you went to sleep. In the dark, when the only light in our room came from the streetlights outside, and all the creepy porcelain dolls collected on our shelves were shadows, you'd begin, *"In the name of the father, the son, and the Holy Spirit . . ."* You'd then pray for everyone, until you got to me. When you reached me in the roll call, you'd say something like, *"And I pray for the ugliest kid ever born, my sister,"* or *"I pray that my sister can live a long and happy life despite being born with a butt where her face should be."*

Marg, once you said just, *"And I pray for my sister."* I grimaced, waiting to be pelted with my nightly insult, but it never came. I'm not sure if you just fell asleep or if that was some sort of soppy moment, but I always considered it the latter.

Remember that time Mom went on a rampage and combed through everything we owned? She tore our bedroom apart. It was after school called to report we'd both been absent. It was a church day. All our classes were shorter than usual because we had mass. Lots of students skipped rather than spend the day on their knees in the chapel.

You spent that day getting on top of your schoolwork. I spent it smoking weed in some guy's backyard. To our parents, it was the same offense, and we were trialed and grounded equally.

I should have been punished more severely than you were. You were studying. I was smoking weed, eating Goldfish crackers I stole from the corner store. The severity of our punishment was not proportional or fair. You didn't complain about that. You seemed to think you deserved the same punishment as me. Why was that?

I was usually the one getting into trouble. You seemed mostly remorseful that you'd been caught that day. Was that why you didn't complain? Because you held yourself to a higher standard?

I'm not sure why our parents thought we deserved the same punishment. Do you think it had to do with being Catholic? They taught us that murdering rapists who asked for forgiveness on their death beds would be embraced by God in heaven, but the sorry suckers who die unrepentant of lesser sins descend immediately into hell. We were also taught that God condemns trivial things, like slothfulness and gluttony, as grave sins. There isn't enough distinction between the gravity of murder and overeating, in my opinion. Maybe that has something to do with our parents' attitudes.

The whole system of penance left me thinking, *If I'm going to sin, I might as well* really *sin*. Why just skip school when I could skip school *and* smoke pot *and* steal Goldfish crackers? Our parents and God would punish me the same way regardless, and I'd be forgiven in bulk, so why not?

When you and I were kids, we always got into fights before going to confession. Do you remember that? We figured we should get our punches in before all our sins were washed away. I remember you pinching me in the pew before going into the booth with the priest. I used to whisper swear words at you before it was my turn. I'd say, *"You're a bitch, Margit."*

"Fuck you."

In the booth with the priest, I'd say, *"Please forgive me for fighting with my sister and for swearing,"* and Father Francis would wave his hand over my head, say a little prayer, and absolve me of all my trespasses.

Our parents were furious when we skipped school. Because Dad didn't finish high school himself, he was always harping on about what a privilege school was and how thankless we were. Maybe that's why we got the same punishment for skipping. It didn't matter to him if we were out giving food to the needy or shooting up heroin— he wanted us in class. Mom found a bag of weed in my sock drawer, and drawings she said were deranged. They were of anthropomorphic sharks eating people. I also drew the structure of a cell, except I drew two cells next to each other, and made them look like boobs. Mom felt that was egregious.

Among your things, she found thong underwear, which might as well have been a sex toy, and some skirts she said were, *"Designed for strippers."* She also found both of our diaries.

It was apparent by what followed that she read your diary cover to cover. She knew minor details of secret dates you'd gone on. She made snide comments about it. She said things like, *"Maybe you should move in with that boy you're secretly dating,"* when you didn't clean up after yourself.

I had read your diary too, but I did so in secret. Because of that, I knew when Mom mentioned the boy you were dating that she had read the whole thing. You didn't mention him until well after page one hundred.

Mom didn't retain anything I wrote in my diary. Shortly after you and I served our sentences, and we were no longer in trouble, I made an offhand comment about a TV show's unrealistic depiction of a mushroom trip. I had written about eating shrooms in my diary. I figured it was public knowledge. I said, *"You know, it's nothing like that."*

Mom gasped. She said, *"What? How would you know?"*

I realized while looking at the frown lines between her eyebrows that she hadn't really read my diary. She must have just skimmed mine. I guess I lost her interest.

———————

Marg, I'm going to list the bright sides to me being dead below. Maybe you can wordsmith this material to recuperate the tone of this note. This hasn't been as upbeat as I intended so far.

Here are some pros to me being dead:

- You can get a tattoo of my name now without it being creepy.

- You can go to Red Lobster more often. My vegetarianism won't hold you back anymore.

- I won't die in a terrible explosion if the person threatening to bomb the building by the Dollar Pal ever actually goes through with it.

- No one will throw pie at you at family events.

- You can all stop worrying about me.

Attempt Thirteen

I want you to know I spent my final months feeling alive. I didn't spend them like a lot of terminal people do, writhing around, sick, doped up, or sleeping. I mostly spent them with that girl I was seeing. She was sort of wild and heedless. We did things like climb up old silos at night and go skinny-dipping. We sped up and down Main Street, belting along to the radio, catcalling men.

We went swimming in a stranger's backyard. They had a heated pool. All the windows in their McMansion were dark. We figured they weren't home. We floated in their steamy pool on our backs with our arms outstretched, ogling the moon.

The pool was fancy. It had cement cherubs surrounding it, and a water feature. While we floated, I told her that when I was a kid, I daydreamed about having a pool. I used to lie in the dead grass in my backyard with my eyes closed tight, picturing a pool noodle under my neck, and the smell of chlorine. No one who ran in our circles had a pool. Pools were reserved for families who could afford luxuries, like name-brand toilet paper, and fridges that dispensed water. When I went swimming, it was at the YMCA, or in that dirty creek behind the hospital.

I gazed up at the night sky, rambling about how life was so unfair. I blabbed on and on about how some people are dealt cards with backyard pools and cherubs, and some people are dealt dirty creeks with leeches. Some people don't even get to swim at all, even at the Y. I wondered aloud what my life might have been like if I had been dealt a better hand. What if I were born in a different place in the world? What if I had some money?

She asked, *"What would you do with the money?"*

I said, *"I don't know. I'd have a pool, I guess."*

She said, *"And why do you want a pool?"*

I said, *"To go swimming, obviously."*

She dipped her hair back in the water and said, *"You know, we're swimming right now."*

Her dad had just died. She took the year off from art school to grieve in Drysdale. Shortly after her dad passed away, her stepmom uprooted and moved here. Her stepmom couldn't afford the mortgage at their old place without her dad. Compared to some more metropolitan cities, Drysdale is cheap.

Before her dad died, she asked if he had any regrets. He said yes. He then advised her to do whatever she wanted. Tell people to fuck off more. Take what you want. Stir shit up.

I'm not sure whether I'd give the same advice. I will say I don't regret spending my last days with someone who was acting on whims, living for herself. I think it is important to tell people off sometimes, and to do things that make you feel happy—like go swimming. I think there is something sage in saying that sometimes you ought to take what you want.

Other people take what they want all the time. I believe we only live once. I'll try to send you a sign if that isn't the case, but I'm fairly certain this is it. We get one life. If I didn't jump in some stranger's fancy pool, I'd have died never floating next to a cement cherub at midnight.

It mattered more that I sucked what I could out of my remaining existence than it did that I was trespassing, right? Or am I wrong? Maybe I'm wrong. I didn't always have the best judgment.

I think her dad was on morphine when he gave her his advice. He had cancer. It was advanced. I think he was in a lot of pain. Maybe he wasn't thinking straight.

She *definitely* wasn't thinking straight. She was out of her mind. I think she was devastated by her dad's death and confused. She felt anonymous in Drysdale. She did dangerous things because no one here knew her.

She would check if car doors were open, steal things like buttons from cup holders, and the rosaries hanging from rearview windows. She pulled them apart, and used the beads to make art. She had this colossal canvas in her bedroom with trash stuck to it. It looked like an explosion. It had this bright yellow circle painted in the middle, and this burst of beads, buttons, feathers, and trash surrounding it.

She'd steal political signs off lawns and throw them off the over-pass.

I once saw her key a cop car.

She often drove with her eyes closed.

In a lot of ways, she reminded me of Greta. They were both big readers. They were always referencing writers, politicians, and activists I'd never heard of. They had similar principles, and were impassioned by topics like voting, and what was on the news.

I wish I could have introduced them. I think they would have made good friends.

She and I ate caviar a few towns over. Neither of us had ever tried it before. I usually tried to eat vegan, but she talked me into it. She didn't know I was planning on dying, but said, *"Come on. We can't die without trying caviar."* I took that as a sign from the universe that I had to eat it.

I didn't like it, but she did. She ate most of it.

After we finished, we snuck out without paying. That same night, she schmoozed these middle-aged men into buying us drinks at a dive bar and then ghosted them. We ran outside, sloshed for free. We ripped branches from someone's pine tree, wove them into wreaths, then made out in a cemetery with pine crowns on our heads.

Some of that might sound sort of shitty. Maybe it was shitty. I don't know. I had a good time with her. In fact, I spent almost every moment with her smiling. Regardless of whether you take issue with trespassing, keying cop cars, or petty theft, I want you to know I enjoyed myself. It's nice to know that someone was happy before they died, right?

I was happy before I died.

Attempt Fourteen

If you see Greta, tell her I remembered camping. I used to go with her and her parents. It wasn't backwoods camping. We went to the type of campground that had a tuckshop, a grimy outdoor wading pool, and spots to toss horseshoes. There were mosquitos and trees, but it felt less like being in the bush than it did like visiting a seasonal trailer park. Families lived in their rusty RVs and pop-up campers from June until September. Some built porches off their RVs and decorated. They hung flags, Christmas lights, and tacky signs that said things like HAPPY CAMPERS.

Tell her I often thought about the first time we went. It was the summer after ninth grade. I felt like a lost animal released in an unfamiliar ecosystem; like I was a caught badger, driven miles away from my habitat, freed in a forest I'd never badgered in before. I had only ever existed in my house, my family, my school, my neighborhood, my town. My family didn't have the money to go any-where.

Growing up, Greta was always allowed to invite one friend to come camping. She told me that when she invited me. Because of that, I knew being asked was special. It meant I was her best friend.

We bought candy at the tuckshop and roamed around the campgrounds, sucking on sour keys until our tongues felt raw. I looked at the campers surrounding us like they were alien creatures in a zoo. There were packs of wild kids running barefoot through the dirt. There were shirtless middle-aged dads with round, stiff bellies tossing cardboard beer boxes into campfires. The women wore stained, oversized T-shirts, or splash pants over one-piece bathing suits. They used their sunglasses like headbands to get their hair out of their eyes.

These people weren't radically different from my family. Just a little. We were socio-economically comparable; we watched the same TV shows, spoke the same language, ate the same Pop-Tarts. They were just more uninhibited, unapologetically trashy, and seemingly happier. If my family were woodland creatures, we were a pack of badgers who lived under a shed in a subdivision and ate junk from suburban garbage bins. These campers were also badgers, but they lived free in the forest, where they ate mushrooms and worms. The subtle social differences shocked me.

There was a sort of campground commune culture. Everyone nodded and waved like they were neighbors. Adults scolded children who weren't theirs. All the kids who camped there saw each other every summer. Everyone knew each other.

The first day there, a kid approached me when Greta was in the bathroom. I was standing outside, picking a dandelion apart. He said, "So, you're Greta's new best friend?"

I shrugged. "I guess so."

He said, "Lucky."

When we rode our bikes by campsites, I heard kids cooing, "Is that Greta?" It felt like she was some sort of celebrity there. They all knew her. They were all excited to see her. I felt proud she was my friend.

At our high school, there was a clear social divide. Popular kids weren't friends with kids who weren't considered cool. In fact, they were pretty cruel to them. They made disgusted faces when unpopular kids were paired with them for projects. It was normal to use the bathroom and to hear some girl crying in a stall because she'd been bullied by Hayley Scott.

At school, Greta and I were sort of middle-class. We weren't ostracized, but we weren't popular. Things were different at the campsite. Greta was cool there. She didn't act like the cool kids at school, though. She was nice. She said "Hey!" to every kid we passed. She invited everyone to hang out with us.

I returned to the campgrounds with her family every summer for the rest of high school. I found the whole experience enlightening. In addition to learning how to cook banana boats and pie iron pizza on a campfire, I learned that the way our school operated wasn't the only way the world could work. People could be kind to each other regardless of status. It also helped me understand that in different settings, with different casts of people, our roles in life could change.

At one point, Greta and I were standing in a clearing in the woods with a pack of kids. We were all dirty, dusty, and covered in bug bites. They wanted to play Manhunt.

The teenagers we knew back home were over playing childish games like Manhunt. They were mature; they occupied themselves with house parties and talking about the future. The campsite teenagers weren't talking about the future. They were present in the moment we were in. They wanted to play hide-and-seek.

I remember being little. I remember looking in the mirror and seeing my face as a kid. I had uneven bangs. I remember my flat child chest, and how my hips were shaped before puberty. I remember feeling threads in my gums break when I had a wobbly tooth, and the intense allegiance I felt to other children. I remember seeing adults as the other, as a group I wasn't a part of. I thought I had waited as long as I could to jump ship from the kids' boat to the grown-ups'. I thought of the kids who jumped early as turncoats. I thought they were traitors who abandoned their Barbies for makeup and jeans. I knew we all had to jump ship at one point, but I wanted to wait until the last possible moment. When we were camping, I questioned if I had jumped early. I remember playing Manhunt, riding on the back of Greta's bike, soaring down a gravel road at dusk, and thinking, *Holy shit, I'm still a kid here.*

Places in town reminded me of Greta. The mall. The train bridge. The high school. I thought of her when I saw teenaged girls, people riding bicycles, and whenever I smelled bug spray. She and I drifted apart about a year ago. We were best friends throughout all of high school, but we grew apart after classes ended. We weren't in school together every day anymore. We started hanging out with different people. Friendships change when people grow up, I guess.

Every time we went camping, I felt like I saw this glimpse of who Greta was before she was a teenager. She was a more carefree version of herself at the campgrounds. If you see her, tell her I always thought of her that way. At our school in Drysdale, she was jaded. She seemed older. The campgrounds seemed to rejuvenate her.

I wondered sometimes if maybe she and I were only meant to be friends for that phase of our lives. Sometimes I thought she and I caught each other right on the cusp of leaving our childhoods, so the bits of us that were still kids could cling to each other for the last moments before our boats sank.

Greta, I doubt you'll read this. If you do, though, I want you to know that I always cared about you. I associated you with running around town, laughing. I thought of riding on the back of your bike at dusk. No matter where we were, I always saw you as Campgrounds Greta.

Attempt Fifteen

I considered getting my last rites. Not because I felt particularly Catholic, but because I had done most of the other sacraments. I was baptized. I had my first Communion. Penance. I was confirmed. I never liked the feeling when I didn't finish something. For example, it bugged me that I didn't graduate high school.

I bet you didn't know that. Whenever people talked about high school around me, I sensed they thought I didn't care. Marg often made snide comments about it. When I asked for a favor, she'd say, *"Sorry, I only do that for people with high school diplomas."* I don't think she knew she was rubbing salt in a wound. She probably considered her occasional jab an appropriate penance.

Everything I cared about was tangled up like a potted plant's rotted roots. You wouldn't know without studying my yellowed leaves that I was secretly twisted up. I figured it was bad enough for me to fail high school, it would be worse to burden everyone with me being miserable about it. I thought the least I could do was pretend I didn't care.

The truth is, I cared when I didn't finish something. I didn't just want to check things off a list, however. I wanted to finish things really, truly, fully. If I watched a movie, for example, and I missed bits, I didn't consider it truly watched. If I drove through a city and I didn't stop, or I just stopped for gas, or for lunch, I wouldn't say I'd been there.

It's a shame I couldn't get the whole collection of sacraments; however, I couldn't collect them all anyway. It's impossible for anyone to. Priests can never get the sacrament of marriage. Married people and women can never be ordained. Everyone dies at least one short.

Collecting the sacraments would be at odds with my principles anyway. I had quite a few grievances with the Catholic Church. I know that's a sensitive topic for some of you. If Marg were here, she'd be nudging my ribs.

I considered going to confession to be absolved of my sins before dying. Not because I bought into that. I would just be doing it for my mom and dad to feel at peace. If you think they might like to hear I went to confession, and you're okay with lying, tell them I went. I'd rather not actually trouble a priest with my trespasses.

Despite not believing anyone can truly absolve me of anything, I do think there is something cathartic to fessing up to mistakes you've made, and having someone tell you *it's okay, you're forgiven*. So, if you don't mind, I'd like to confess to a few things now. Maybe, if anyone is reading, you can forgive me. If no one is reading, that's okay too. It'll be nice to get these off my chest, regardless.

For years, I told everyone I had irritable bowel syndrome, but I didn't. It was an excuse I kept in my back pocket to leave social situations early. I used it to disappear from parties, bars, and people's houses. I spent a lot of time in bathrooms on my phone. I left Jerry's birthday party early last year. When people texted me, Where did you go? I replied, ibs, and they understood. Rather than stay somewhere unhappily, I would get up. I'd say, *"Excuse me, I have irritable bowel syndrome,"* and I would leave to go do something I preferred.

I'm sorry for lying to you about that.

I once stole a twenty-dollar bill from Dad's wallet. He'd taken it out to order us a pizza. We had to eat plain spaghetti with butter and parmesan that night instead. Dad was so angry he lost the twenty, he pitched a fit. He hurled a glass cup against the kitchen wall. He thought the twenty fell out of his pocket at the ATM, or that he had been pickpocketed. I remember sitting in the quiet aftermath of his tantrum, hearing the clink of Mom sweeping up shards of broken glass. Marg choked down her pasta like it was poisoned, occasionally shooting me dirty looks—as if she knew what I did. I felt a heartbeat in my pocket where the twenty was.

I'm sorry for stealing.

I also regularly stole from the Dollar Pal. I never took money, but I took things. I pinched toilet paper from the staff room, and I stole merchandise. I am not sorry that I took necessities like light bulbs, tampons, and toothpaste, because I was poor, but I am sorry that I also took a water gun, a fake sunflower, gum, a plastic lizard, bubbles, and a dinosaur coloring book.

When I was thirteen, Jerry called things off with her boyfriend Harry because she found lesbian porn in her computer's search history.

Margit and I were at her house when they broke up. Our parents had been fighting. We watched Harry leave with a duffel bag on his shoulder and tears in his eyes. He said, "See you later, kiddos."

I liked Harry. He made Marg and me butterscotch pudding. He liked to watch nature shows, and Jerry thought he was funny. She was always laughing when he was around.

My mom came over after he left. She and Jerry griped about how disgusting men are, while we all watched romantic comedies and ate mint chocolate chip ice cream. Jerry ended up dating a man with a brown tooth and blurry tattoos on his forearms after Harry.

I'm sorry, Jerry. As you likely now suspect, Harry was innocent. The culprit was me.

This is connected to my last confession in that it's related to lying and lesbianism.

I dated a woman named Gwen for a brief period about two years ago. She was one of the only three people on the "women interested in women" side of the dating apps in Drysdale at the time.

It was not a meaningful relationship on my end; however, Gwen felt differently. She took us seriously. She made a photo of her and I dancing her Facebook profile picture. Drysdale is a small town, and that caused a bit of a stir. You might recall, it was sensational gossip. My mom heard about it through the ladies at work.

She confronted me. She said, *"Are you seriously dating a woman?"*

I said, *"What do you mean seriously?"*

I was thinking of breaking things off with Gwen.

Mom said, *"You're not gay."*

She said that so definitively that for a moment, I thought, *Oh shit, am I not gay?*

I said, *"I'm bi,"* and she rolled her eyes.

I think she thought I was just trying to get a rise out of her. As if I were dating Gwen just to be exasperating. She didn't believe I was really bi.

She was right. I wasn't. I was a lesbian. I said I was bi because I figured that might be preferable. My mom could still believe I would end up with a man. My dad's limited worldview that women orbit men could be less rocked. This is an example of one of my miscalculated attempts at politeness. I thought pretending to be bisexual was more courteous than fessing up to being a lesbian. Marg was always telling me to take the path of least resistance. I just wanted to make things easier for everyone.

I apologize to bisexuals for masquerading as you, to lesbians for denying you, as well as to any man who thought I might have been sexually attracted to him.

These confessions are all lousy, aren't they?

Attempt Sixteen

I held out on you in that last attempt. I was confessing to half-assed sins. I've thought of some meatier ones. Use these instead, okay, Marg?

I went on a transatlantic trip last year and I didn't tell anyone. That's why I stood up my own birthday party. I was secretly in France. I got a little unexpected cash from my tax return, and on a whim, I used it to buy a dirt-cheap ticket to Paris.

I'd never traveled anywhere before. I wanted to fly somewhere. Visiting cities forty minutes away from Drysdale always felt like an adventure. Going to France felt like going to the moon. I was worried I might get lost, or human trafficked somehow. I had never been on a plane before. I didn't know anyone who traveled. I had to ride a bus out of town to get to the airport. The bus was crammed full of old ladies migrating to Florida. I was so anxious, one of the ladies asked me why my leg was shaking. I told her I had some illness that made me jittery, to avoid having to admit out loud that I felt nervous.

It all turned out to be easier than I thought it would be. I made it to the airport in one piece. I accidentally left a water bottle in my carry-on, which swiftly got confiscated, both my ears popped on the plane, and I worried I was riding the subway backward, but I made it to my hostel.

I should have told someone I was going. If I had somehow been human trafficked or gotten into an accident, or lost, I'd have left you all with quite the puzzle. It would seem like I had just up and vanished. I'd end up being the main character in some cold case documentary.

Despite regretting not telling anyone, I'm glad I went. I had fun. I met an Irish person who was also there alone. Their name was Rabbit. I asked if their name was really Rabbit, and they said, *"Yes, but it wasn't always. I renamed myself."* I wondered what their name was before, but sensed it was impolite to ask. We wandered around together by the Eiffel Tower the first night. It was lit up and twinkling. We got crepes from a stand and smoked thin cigarettes by a gaudy fountain.

Rabbit told me about Limerick, where they were from, and I told them about Drysdale. They invited me to visit them, and I invited them to visit me, but I warned them that Drysdale was not much of a tourist destination. I said they should only come if they wanted to feel jaded, be hatecrimed, or if they had a hankering to try fentanyl in a basement.

We got lost trying to find our way back to our hostel. It's what I worried about most, getting lost. I worked myself up about it. The streets weren't a grid, but all interwoven. Rabbit wasn't anxious. I tried to hide that I was because I didn't want to be a downer, but I felt panicked. Rabbit could tell, despite my best efforts. They said, *"Hey, everything will be fine. We'll find our way."*

I wasn't used to being calmly assured of anything, let alone that I would find my way. I'd grown up in a house full of tightly wound people who lost their cool easily. I couldn't recall a time when I felt lost or worried and it wasn't a cause for hysterics. I didn't know it was possible to face stresses the way Rabbit did. It hadn't occurred to me that not panicking was an option.

We sat on a bench after wandering for over an hour. We almost resolved to sleep there before realizing the bench was miraculously right across the street from our hostel. We both gasped when we noticed it, then looked at each other and laughed.

We shared our room with five other strangers. They were already asleep by the time we got in. I was so tired I passed out in my clothes. The next morning, Rabbit jostled me awake and asked if I wanted to go to Versailles with them.

We bought these chocolate pastries at a café before taking the train together. They had figured out the tickets and had written notes on where to go. I followed them like they were the star of Bethlehem. They were nice to me. They knew it was my first trip anywhere, took me under their wing, and didn't seem annoyed—even though I'm certain I was annoying. They had tips from their research about how to avoid large crowds in the palace. We were climbing stairs that didn't look like they were for the public and dipping into areas that might have been reserved.

It seems ridiculous now, but I was so impressed by Rabbit. I felt anchored to my insular small town and brainwashed by our attitude that going anywhere was hard. Going to the airport felt massive to me. I was overwhelmed. Seeing someone my age capable of independently navigating a new place felt like seeing someone offhandedly perform a miracle.

When we were outside in the palace gardens, Rabbit told me all this history they knew. They told me Marie Antoinette had a jeweled horseshoe put in her mouth to straighten her teeth. They told me all about dentistry in the 1700s—like how often people had to get their teeth yanked, and when toothpaste was invented. They were very well-informed about the history of dentistry, for some reason.

While we walked, and I learned about incisors, I thought about how I was standing in places Marie Antoinette had. I was looking at her things, strolling over her checkered tile in my grimy sneakers. To be honest, I didn't know much about Marie Antoinette. As we know, I didn't pay much attention in school. I probably would have felt the same way about any historical person plucked out of time. It was just the idea that a supposedly fascinating person, who lived and died years ago, existed in the spots I stood. I felt sort of reborn, sensing how both enormous and puny the world was at that moment. Rabbit looked at me and grinned in a way I think signaled that they felt the same way—though in retrospect, they may have just been showing me their teeth.

I'm not sorry I went on that trip, but I am sorry I didn't tell anyone about it. That was irresponsible. I didn't want to be told not to go. I didn't want Mom or Dad to say it was a bad use of my tax return, or for Jerry to say it was dangerous, or for anyone to freak me out about it. I just wanted to go.

Nothing was ever as simple as I wished it were. There's this domino effect to every haphazard choice we make. We're all in this web together. Because I didn't tell anyone I went to France, I accidentally ditched my own birthday party. I totally forgot about it. Everyone was so mad at me. I couldn't explain myself.

I just wanted to be happy, but sometimes your own happiness comes at the expense of other people's, doesn't it? It's hard to balance being both happy and considerate. I often tried to be both by lying, but that usually made it worse.

I lied about why I didn't graduate high school. I said it was because I was lazy and I didn't do my homework. I said I was preoccupied with skipping class to smoke weed. That wasn't the whole truth. I did skip class to smoke weed sometimes, but I also did most of my homework. At first I was afraid to hand it in. Margit had done most of my homework in earlier years, and I knew she was a better writer.

I struggled to focus. I think I had attention deficit disorder, or something. I was always daydreaming. I felt restless in class. Mom and Dad weren't particularly book smart, so they couldn't help me. Dad didn't graduate high school, and Mom just scraped by, but Margit loved to read. I used to joke that she was adopted because I don't know where she came from. Her teachers put gold star stickers on her assignments. Her homework was held up as the good example in class. To her credit, she tried to help me with my schoolwork, but she was controlling. She always took over completely when she tried to help.

After she moved out, I tried to mimic her writing style. While there was a noticeable decline in my grades, no teachers caught onto why. My marks were worse, but overall, I was doing okay. I was passing. I had to pass my final English assignment to complete the class and graduate. It was a paper about *Hamlet*. While I pored over my notes, I thought about how I had to finish twelfth grade to move on to the next stage of my life. To escape Drysdale, I needed to get into college. I had no money to move away without student loans. I had applied to three schools and was wait-listed at two. Rejected at one. While I read *Hamlet*, I started to think a little too much about how I was a teenager, and how soon I'd become an adult. I felt like I was on a sinking ship again.

I was supposed to have studied *Romeo and Juliet* in ninth grade, *Macbeth* in tenth grade, and *A Midsummer Night's Dream* in eleventh, but I hadn't. Margit had. *Hamlet* was the first Shakespeare I had ever actually read, and I didn't get it. I remember reading that "To be, or not to be" speech, and thinking, *What the fuck does this mean?*

I hesitated. I wanted more time to consider the repercussions of not reading the Shakespeare plays I was supposed to by my age. I wanted more time to figure out my next step. I wanted to stay on the boat I was on. I felt like I had just gotten on it. I didn't feel ready to hop onto a new one yet. I wanted more time to understand *Hamlet.*

I didn't hand in my final essay because I choked. I know that's a shoddy reason not to hand it in, and to fail high school, but it's the truth. I should have just handed a draft in, prayed I passed, and got out of there, but I didn't.

I'm not sure why I lied about this. I usually lie in an attempt to be polite, I think. That's what Marg always told me to do. I said I had IBS, for example, so that I didn't have to say that I was tired of someone's company. I said I was bisexual to appease people. I didn't mention going to France because I knew everyone would say I shouldn't go and would be worried about me. I didn't want to needlessly ruffle feathers.

That's not why I lied about high school. I didn't lie about that to be polite. I guess sometimes I lied for no good reason, or for reasons that just served me. Before I died, I was seeing that girl, and I lied to her every time I saw her.

For one, she misheard me when I told her my name. We met in that thrift store off Main Street. I was tilting my head, looking down at a photo plaque of Meryl Streep. She approached me while I considered buying the photo. She said, *"Are you a fan of Meryl's?"* in a tone that I could tell also meant, *Are you gay?*

I nodded and she said, *"Me too."*

She then told me her name. I told her my name was Sigrid, but she misheard me. She thought I said, "Astrid." I should have corrected her, but I didn't. Not because I felt tongue-tied or anxious—I just felt like pretending. I took the opportunity to lie.

I wanted to try on being a different person. I was feeling bad for myself. I was insecure about my menial job, not going to school and moving away. I thought maybe I'd have fun pretending to be someone different. I also thought it was unlikely for someone to like me if I were just myself.

She typed my name as "Astrid" in her phone, and we started texting. I put on a sort of Astrid persona, pretending I was saving up to move to the East Coast, even though I wasn't. I said I wanted to be a writer, even though I was terrible at it. I told her my favorite book was *The Iliad*, but I'd never read it. I didn't even know what it was about. Is it about a flower? I had seen it in a stack of Margit's schoolbooks. I said I had no social media because I cared about internet privacy. I blocked her on every platform, and as an extra precaution, I changed my profile pictures to scenery without my face in it.

I don't know why I did any of that. I liked her, and I felt bad that I had been so dishonest. By the time I realized I had made a mess of things, it was too late for me to fix it. It became a headache. I was always worried I would run into someone in town who knew me, and who would refer to me as "Sigrid" in front of her. Whenever she'd meet me at the Dollar Pal, I had to stealthily remove my name tag.

She picked me up every time there was a bomb threat. She didn't have a job, so she was often bored, and always wanted to hang out. She was seemingly happy I kept getting unplanned days off. Once, a cop who had spoken to me during previous evacuations stopped me on my way to her car. Her window was rolled down. I worried he'd say my real name within earshot of her.

Thankfully, he didn't. He said, *"Have you seen anything suspicious?"* I said no.

I always said no to the cops. The truth is I saw a lot of suspicious things. In fact, there were specific people I suspected might be behind the threats.

There was this one guy who came in the store at noon a few times a week to grab his lunch. He went to Adult Ed in the building. I noticed him because we went to high school together. He dropped out, like I did. When we were teenagers, he and I occasionally smoked weed together. There was one night, when I was with him, Greta, and a crowd of kids. He said he didn't want to go to school the next day. We all agreed. None of us wanted to go. That night, we all watched him call the school from a pay phone and leave a message. He said someone was planning to bring a gun to school the next day. School was canceled. It made the local news.

It became difficult to gauge which lies were acceptable. Sometimes lying feels like pretending. It's harmless—like April Fools'. It's fun. It's kinder to lie sometimes, right? Lying can make people feel better. We tell people they look good, when they don't. We tell people we like the food they cooked, when we didn't. There are other lies that cross a line, though. Brazen, shameless lies that could hurt somebody. I think this was one of those.

When I saw him in the store, we talked about how he was going back to school. He said he wanted to better himself. He wanted to go to college. Get a job. Become a lawyer, maybe. It would be strange for him to take the initiative to return to school just to send out false bomb threats, but he did have a history of taking similar extreme measures to play hooky. I often wondered if he made the threats.

There are government offices in that building. That's where people get employment services, like social security and disability support. A lot of Drysdale residents live in poverty. The place is rife with unemployment. There used to be a bunch of car factories on the outskirts of town, but most have closed in the last decade or so. Now we just have vacant buildings.

There are many people around town who moan about residents who rely on government assistance. On the first of the month, when people get their government checks, it's hard to get through the day without hearing someone quip that McDonald's, Walmart, and the Dollar Pal are going to be busy. There was one customer who, like clockwork, said, *"I'm glad our taxes pay for their Big Macs."* He said, *"You know why it's so busy in your store today, right?"*

I tried not to engage with him. I scanned his items and gritted my teeth, but still—he habitually ranted to me about government handouts and his precious tax dollars. He seemed fanatical. Once, after a bomb threat, he joked, *"I hope someone does eventually bomb that place for real."* I wouldn't be shocked to learn he was calling in the threats to disrupt the social services, to stick it to the poor people.

I didn't tell the cops about any of my suspicions because I didn't like the cops. I had a number of problematic run-ins with them as a teenager. Once, a cop stole my lighter. I didn't even have weed on me, let alone a cigarette. He said I had no business with it. I said he had no right to take it, but he did anyway.

The girl I was seeing didn't like cops either. She called them "The Pigs."

I always wondered why calling cops "pigs" was disparaging. I'd rather be a pig than a cop. Pigs are adorable. If anything, it's a compliment. If I walked around town and everyone called me a pig, I'd think, *This is amazing*. It would feel like we were all playing some cute make-believe game.

I wish adults did things like pretend to be pigs more often. I remember being a kid and approaching other kids, saying, "Hi, I'm a dinosaur," and them roaring with me without any reluctance. We had this shared understanding. I felt connected to people.

I found it easier to relate to people when we could be dinosaurs. I found it harder to click with others as I got older. I worried I didn't think the same way other adults thought. I worried I might be abnormal or stunted.

Even when I was little, I struggled to play with some kids. Marg and I didn't play well together, for one. I never liked playing house, styling my dolls' hair, or pretending to be an adult. I didn't want to play that I was a mother, a wife, a teacher, or a nurse. I didn't want to imagine there were bad guys after me, or something to run from. I preferred happy games. I wanted to be a goblin.

For me, being grown-up felt similar to playing a board game without understanding the instructions. It wasn't a colorful, jazzy board game either. It wasn't Candyland, Chutes and Ladders, or Hungry Hungry Hippos. It was all math and rules—a lifeless, restrictive game that I wasn't good at, and I didn't understand.

I used to spend all my spare time rooting through my imagination. My bed was never a bed. It was a castle. It was a boat. When I looked up at the ceiling, I imagined the world was upside down. When I ate ice cream, I stirred it until it melted, and pretended I was shoveling mud into my mouth. I was rarely myself. I was a necromancer. I was a shark. A monster. I couldn't wait to get home from school, descend to the basement, and hold a Barbie.

Where does that creativity go, I wonder? Why do we lose that?

I'm not sure I did lose it, to be honest. I think maybe I still had the drive to make believe, but I had no good way to channel it. It was misfiring inside me. Maybe I lied to that girl I was seeing to feel like I did with my toys. Maybe I was trying to hold myself like a doll. Maybe I was weaving a make-believe story for myself, as if I were a Barbie, not a human, and without considering that she was a person too. On my end, it felt less like lying than it did like playing. At first, I found it fun.

I just wanted to be another person. I found it difficult to be myself. It's easier to pretend to be someone else than it is to be my real, authentic self. There are fewer stakes. When I'm not myself and people reject me, or I don't fit in, I don't have to take it personally. They weren't really rejecting *me*. Being my real self makes me more vulnerable. When I operate in life as if I'm playing a game, losing feels less significant. I can just start over. Play again.

I don't think I lied about failing high school for fun. I don't think that lie was like the Astrid lie. It was never entertaining to claim I failed because I didn't try, or because I skipped class to smoke weed. It was just less embarrassing to say that than it was to explain that I failed because I didn't understand *Hamlet*.

I have never been particularly good at explaining myself. Sometimes, I thought it was better to lie to spare people having to endure my attempt to explain myself. Maybe that's a cop-out. Maybe I told myself that because it served me to think that way.

It's hard for me to understand when a lie is better than the truth. I understand, in theory, why it can be better to lie to spare someone's feelings, or to make people comfortable. In practice, however, it's tough for me to gauge how other people feel, or what might make them feel comfortable. Margit was always the one who was good at that.

I think knowing some lies were okay set me up to lie to satisfy myself. I felt better saying I failed high school because I didn't try. I said my name was Astrid for fun. I prefer black-and-white rules. I would prefer to be told to never lie, rather than be told I should lie sometimes. I think when rules are gray, we think about them too much. Nothing is really right or wrong, or good or bad when you think about it too much.

Generally, I prefer honesty. When you lie, you have to uphold the lie with more lies. It can get so complicated. You end up doing things like missing your own birthday party and hiding your name tag at work. You risk upsetting people.

I don't know which lies I should ask forgiveness for right now. I used to be dragged to confession all the time when I was a kid. The school would bring our classes once a month, and Mom took me and Marg sometimes. I remember sitting with Father Francis, admitting to a list of my transgressions, and then worrying as I did my penance that I had missed something. I knew how to confess to sins like stealing and pinching Margit, but I didn't know how to confess to sins that felt cloudier. For example, I often lied to my parents to spare Margit. She and I fought a lot, and she was stronger than me, and sometimes she really hurt me. My parents would storm into our bedroom, in swamp-monster form, and I would pretend it was an accident. I would say, "Margit didn't do anything wrong."

Was lying then still a sin if I lied so she wouldn't get hurt? I have no idea. Life would have been a lot easier for me if I could have just been honest.

I lied earlier when I mentioned Greta. I pretended not to know why we weren't friends anymore. I know why. It's because she developed an opioid addiction. She and I snorted OxyContin off a butter knife for the first time together in a garage two summers ago. The garage owner had just had his wisdom teeth yanked. His orthodontist gave him a prescription. When he offered it to us, I said yes before Greta did. She followed my lead.

At that time, Greta and I were both feeling sort of listless. We'd finished high school. She graduated, but she didn't get accepted into the only school she applied to. It had this social work program she had set her heart on. I'd moved out of my parents' house and was working at the Dollar Pal, watching the seasonal aisle change from Halloween, to Thanksgiving, to Christmas, to Easter, and back again. Greta was living with her mom, going to adult ed, and studying to bump her average up so she could reapply to that school.

Everyone we grew up with had gone to college or trade school, had gotten pregnant, or was planning their next big move. Greta and I spent a lot of our time feeling sorry for ourselves. We used to smoke by the high school at night, like we were ghosts anchored there still. I accepted the oxy without putting much thought into it. Maybe deep down something inside me wanted to dabble more with self-sabotage, but mostly I think I was just bored.

Greta kept doing it. It was strange. When it started, I thought she was sort of cosplaying as a Drysdale drug addict. I didn't take it seriously. I thought she was sort of putting it on.

Despite feeling aimless, I still believed Greta and I would figure everything out. We would get out of Drysdale. She would eventually get into college. Everything would be okay. Every time she snorted dust off a key in front of me, I thought of it as a joke. I thought she was just trying to understand what it felt like to be the character she was playing. Maybe one day when she was a social worker, or a professor, or a politician, she would draw understanding from this blip in time when she pretended to be someone else.

When I was a kid in the basement, I channeled Jo. I experienced the toy world through her perspective. My voice was hers when I spoke. When I played with other toys, I considered them side characters. I put on voices that weren't mine for them. Occasionally I tried channeling other toys. I held my stuffed unicorn Francine and tried on her personality. I looked around the toy world, pretending I was her. Doing that gave me a deeper understanding of the place. I would rearrange the gardens so Francine could more easily graze through them. I would identify the toys that Francine was closest with and sit them nearer to each other. Over time, I did that for all my toys, but I always came back to channel Jo.

When I was a teenager, I tried on different personalities. I think that's common, right? When you're not sure who you are yet, it makes sense to pretend to be someone to see what suits you best, or to figure out which version of you can operate through the world easiest. I changed how I dressed. I cut my hair. I tried listening to different genres of music. I once took up jogging. I thought maybe I was supposed to be athletic. Maybe I was supposed to play guitar.

There are so many options when you're a kid. The world is your oyster, or whatever the saying is. When you're little, you believe you can grow up and become anything. When you get older, the walls start to close in. You can't really pretend to be someone anymore. There's no more experimenting. You are who you are. Trying on new faces when you're not a kid is risky. Masks meld onto your face when you're a grown-up.

Greta started complaining about chronic pain. She said her back was always spasming. She started going to doctors for prescriptions. For months, I was in denial. I considered the situation exasperating. I wanted her to snap out of it. At the time, she didn't look any different. Sometimes she looked a little sleepy, but mostly she looked just like her old self. It was easy to convince myself nothing had changed. She was the same. I tried to talk to her like everything was normal, but it wasn't.

She started showing up at my apartment, and at the Dollar Pal, asking for money. She sold her phone. There was no way to text her. Eventually, she stole fifty dollars from my wallet, and I got angry. We got into an argument. I almost hit her. That fifty was all my money for groceries for two weeks. She said she was sorry, and that she wouldn't do it again. She said, *"You know me, Sig. I would never do that."*

I sensed this horrible vibrational shift. I felt like the sky went black. The sun went out. Every time I was around her, she felt off. She felt like the ghost of her former self. She started to call me incessantly from other people's phones. Eventually, I had to change my number.

I lied earlier partly because I'm not sure who will read this, and I

didn't want to air her dirty laundry. I thought it might be more polite
to lie. I was trying to avoid exposing Greta. I think I was also trying
to protect myself. I struggled to admit this to myself, but Greta was
a drug addict. I think I didn't want you to know that I was culpable
for that. I said yes before she did.

Is it more impolite to expose Greta's situation, or to hide it, when
hiding it also covers me? Or is it self-serving to write about it here, to
get it off my chest, and to ask for forgiveness, at her expense? I don't
know what the right thing to do is.

Marg, when you edit this, can you please help me decipher if it's
better to admit what I did wrong, or if I shouldn't have mentioned
this at all? I find the subject so upsetting, I can't really think about
it clearly.

I guess I lied a lot to protect myself. For example, I lied to most
of you a few months ago when I asked you not to vote for Kevin
Fliner for mayor. I mentioned that I knew him. I said he just gave
me a bad vibe, but that wasn't the whole truth. The whole truth is
more uncomfortable. It was also easier to lie about why I failed high
school. I preferred you all thinking I was lazy rather than exposing
why I really failed. I guess maybe I was just protecting myself from
your reactions.

I prefer the world I built in the basement to reality. I wish real life
were happier and more magical. I wish I could take on a new voice
and be someone else whenever I felt like it. When you play with toys,
you get to imagine scenarios and circumstances. If you don't like the
story you're playing, you can stop, or change it. Everything is altera-
ble. It's made up. If Greta were my doll, I wouldn't play that her life
turned out how it has. I'd brush her hair and start over.

I'd brush my own hair and start over. I'd do things differently. I'd
make things better.

I find it difficult to accept that my life isn't a game, and everything is real and permanent. I have this instinct to pretend things are different, but that doesn't really accomplish anything, does it? I wish things really *were* different.

I am a different person than you are, Marg. I can't always figure out when I should lie and when I shouldn't, like other people can. Can I just be honest with you now? I'm tired of pretending. I don't want to play games.

———————

I don't really have a thoracic aortic aneurysm. I'm sorry for lying to you again. I thought it would make this simpler, but now I realize that maybe I was just trying to make things easier on myself.

The truth is a little more complicated.

Attempt Seventeen

There was a poster in my bedroom with a turtle on it, and the turtle moved. I wondered if the poster was some sort of optical illusion, but it wasn't. It was just a blown-up photo of a turtle in a pond, surrounded by lily pads, and the turtle moved.

I knew turtles in posters couldn't move. I knew that wasn't possible. Despite that, the turtle moved. He was slow, because he was a turtle, but he blinked. He opened his mouth. He turned his neck. There were ripples in the water surrounding him.

When I first noticed movement, I wasn't alarmed. I didn't think much of it, in fact. It didn't stand out to me. It was like seeing leaves fall from a tree. It was like noticing wind.

I started leaving my bedroom to undress because of it. Despite it being a photo, and a photo of a reptile, I felt subconsciously uncomfortable undressing in front of him. Without giving it much thought, I started changing in my bathroom.

One night in the bathroom, when I had one leg in my pajama shorts, it clicked. I recognized that something was off. Posters don't move. I opened my bedroom door and stared at the turtle. I pressed my face up to his face. I watched his eyes for what felt like ten minutes until, finally, he blinked.

When I was a kid, I had a big imagination. When I was in a tree, I was a bird. When I was in a bath, I was an orca. When I played that I was a witch on a broom, not a kid on a bike, I didn't see asphalt beneath me. I saw the sky.

In the basement, my toys were alive. I couldn't differentiate between what was happening in my head and what was real, and I didn't care to. It was normal to climb on the jungle gym, play that it was a pirate's ship, and see dark waves crash where the gravel was.

When we age, and we learn more about the world, and about what's possible and what isn't, we are supposed to start seeing things as they really are. The make-believe fog is supposed to settle, and everything should become real. I think we imagine things when we're kids as practice. It helps prepare us for the possibilities in our future. It's like a dress rehearsal for when we're grown. It lets us explore a world we can control and try on being adults before we really have to be them.

I played with toys longer than most kids did. Marg stopped years before me. I played until I was thirteen, and I didn't stop because I was bored, or because I grew out of it. I just realized that playing with Barbies when you're a teenager is weird. I didn't stop because my Barbies' mouths stopped moving.

For a while, I told myself that I had a kid's imagination because I was still practicing for something. I thought maybe I'd been right when

I was younger. Maybe I really could be anything. Maybe fate had something big in store for me. Maybe I needed more time to imagine things because I was still practicing for something impressive.

Recently I was hanging out with that girl I was seeing. Neither of us had any money. I spent my entire paycheck on rent and bills and lived off my overdraft. She wasn't working and had a bunch of student debt. We couldn't afford to go to the movies or to go out to eat. I was always worried about running into someone I knew with her because she thought my name was Astrid. Because of that, we spent most of our time together roaming Drysdale at night. She spent a lot of time talking about society, and what we thought needed to change. She had never lived in a small town before. She was from a big city. She found Drysdale's politics appalling. The campaign for the city election had started. She and I talked about Kevin Fliner a lot. I told her he was probably going to win, and that riled her up. She wanted to go to his campaign office. Find out where he lived. She wanted to egg his car or light a bag of dog shit on fire on his front porch. She drew little devil horns on pictures of him in the newspaper.

Sometimes she borrowed her stepmom's car, and we sped up and down Main Street, but mostly we wandered around together walking and chatting. We roamed inside the cemetery at night. We smoked weed inside play structures at the park and swung on the swings.

I remember swinging when I was a kid. I remember stretching my legs out as far as I could and thinking every time I swung, I was closer to getting over the bar. I wanted to swing over it, but I never made it. Does anyone ever actually get over the bar? Or is that just something we think we can do when we're kids?

When I went swinging with the girl I was seeing, the chains pressed into my grown hips, and it hurt. I couldn't do it for very long anymore. When I jumped off, I looked down at the gravel beneath me and I swear I saw water. I held my breath when I landed. Rather than skid on the ground, I felt myself sink in an ocean. I gasped a moment after landing, as if my face had bobbed over the sea line. I felt like I was treading water. She asked me if I was okay, and I said, *"Yeah, I just knocked the wind out of myself."*

I was getting older and losing my capacity to imagine. My dress rehearsal was ending, and I was just going to have to be who I was.

I met up with Jerry and Marg at a diner a few months ago. They had cat-shaped salt and pepper shakers on the tables. Jerry asked us to go because she hadn't seen either of us in a while. The last time I saw her, we got into an argument. I think she asked us to meet up partly because she wanted to smooth things over with me, but mostly because she knew Margit and I had drifted apart. Jerry wanted us to be sisters the way she and Mom were.

They called each other almost every night. Jerry was always at our house. She and Mom were best friends. Marg and I weren't really friends, let alone best friends. We were just sisters.

At this point Marg was away at school, reading Renaissance literature, dating college guys. I was working at the Dollar Pal, smoking weed in my apartment, aimlessly roaming around town. Marg and I had nothing to talk about. I didn't really know her anymore. She had grown up and changed. She wasn't the girl who slept in the bunk bed above me. She wasn't the person who yanked my hair when I pissed her off, whose sweaters I stole, or who lied to our parents to save me from being grounded. She'd become this older, worldlier person, and I was left behind. It was exhausting when we were around each other. She was annoyed by and disappointed in me, and I felt abandoned by her. When we were younger, Margit did my homework partly as a charity. She knew I was bad at it. I think she also did it because she was controlling. She would look at my work and say, *"No, that's wrong, let me fix it."*

When she found out I didn't graduate high school, she was angry. She yelled at me. She called me stupid. She and I weren't fighting at this time. A couple years had passed since I'd dropped out, and she was three years into college. We just hardly spoke. We saw each other at holidays and on birthdays. We weren't on bad terms, but we weren't on good ones, either.

At the diner, Marg and Jerry excused themselves to the bathroom. While they were away from our table, I put the cat shakers in front of me. I watched them groom themselves. They had tiny little porcelain tongues that licked their tiny little porcelain paws. The pepper shaker sneezed after she licked the fur between her toes.

When they came back, Jerry asked me if I was okay. I think she and Marg had been talking about me in the bathroom. They both said that I looked tired.

I didn't want to say that I looked tired because there was a sentient poster of a turtle in my bedroom. I didn't want to confess that I'd been staying up late swinging in parks with an insane girl who thought my name was Astrid, or that I'd lost touch with my best friend because she had developed a drug addiction. I was eyeing the twitching salt and pepper shakers in front of me. I knew while I watched them move that I had lost it, so I lied and said that I was fine.

Everyone was always asking me what I planned to do with my life. I couldn't go to a diner with my aunt and sister and just shoot the shit. Almost every conversation I had devolved to discussing my big life plans. I noticed other people my age had a sort of script memorized for themselves. Marg, for example, would say that after her undergraduate degree, she was going to get some other degree in fine arts, and that ultimately, she wanted to be a writer.

I guess that's part of the plight of being young. Everyone around you is fixated on what you're going to do next. *How are you going to set up your life? What are you going to school for? How are you going to make money? What are you working toward? Will you get married? Will you have kids?*

I shoveled French toast into my face, wondering if I had accidentally taken an edible. I was watching the saltshaker groom itself, while Marg said, *"And what about you, Sig?"*

Jerry said, *"Yeah, what are your big life plans?"*

On my first day of kindergarten, I sat in a short orange chair at a circular table surrounded by other kids. There was a bouquet of crayons in the center of the table. Our teacher instructed us to draw what we wanted to be when we grew up. Most kids drew ballerinas, athletes, race car drivers, and that sort of thing. I drew a great white shark. I remember my teacher telling me I couldn't be an animal, animals weren't occupations, but that she liked the creativity.

My parents put my shark drawing on the fridge. It was there for years. It became a family joke that I wanted to be a fish. They couldn't tell that it was a drawing of a shark, and I felt too humbled by the situation to correct them. I just went along with it. I laughed with them. I made a fish face by sucking in my cheeks and puckering my lips.

I got a shark tattooed to my chest last year. To be honest, I didn't put that much thought into why I got it. I just thought it looked cool. In retrospect, I think it meant something. I always wanted to be something I couldn't be.

Recently I was having a bath, and looked down at my body in the water. My chest and stomach looked paler than usual. I looked into the eyes of my tattoo to see if it would blink. It didn't, but sharks don't have eyelids. They just have this membrane that closes before they bite something. While inspecting my tattoo, I noticed slits along my ribs. It looked as if I had been slashed with a big hunting knife, or something. I felt my skin there and inhaled, and I swear— it felt like I was breathing through gills.

I know I couldn't breathe through gills. I know that I imagined that; however, something was obviously wrong with me. I didn't know how long I would have before I stopped knowing what was real and what wasn't. I had cracked. I was going insane.

I always had a big imagination, but you can't have a big imagination when you grow up—unless you're using it to design video games, or write fantasy novels, or something. It's not normal to be an adult and to think the way I did. I was nuts. I think if it went on, you might have found me dead, floating face-first in a creek, thinking I could breathe there. That would be worse than this, right? I didn't want to die screaming that I was a fish.

Like everyone in their early twenties, the girl I was seeing talked a lot about what she wanted to do with her future too. Unlike Margit, she hadn't memorized her speech yet. She was still struggling to write it.

Once, we were trespassing on a stranger's farm outside town. It had just gotten dark. She was whispering about her dreams while we skulked past a herd of nosy cows. She said she wasn't sure if she wanted to become an animator, a graphic designer, or if she should just paint things and hope they sell. She considered that maybe she should get into tattooing. Or maybe become a political radical. Fuck shit up. She wondered if she should drop out of school. She asked me what I thought.

The cows were drawing attention to us. They crowded by the fence we walked beside. A few of them mooed.

I whispered, *"Well, you know what they say? To thine own self be true, or whatever."*

When I was pretending to be Astrid, I always said shitty things like that. I tried to sound smart, like I read *Hamlet*.

We were planning to climb up an old silo. We couldn't think of anything to do, glanced around, and saw the silo in the skyline.

She asked me what I wanted to be. I was pretending to be Astrid, so I wrote a speech for her. I said I wanted to write picture books about sharks. I suggested maybe she could be the illustrator.

While she ran with that idea, I saw the sky open. In the dark clouds, I saw God's old man face frown down at me. I jumped and looked at her, to see if she saw him too, but she didn't. She wasn't paying attention. She was busy rubbing her hands on her shirt, preparing to climb up the side of the silo.

I followed behind her. The ladder was old and rusty. It was made of these metal steps that were welded into the side of the cement. Some of the steps were deformed.

Despite the run-down state of the ladder, we climbed all the way up the silo. My hands got sweaty near the top. Once she reached the last step, I hovered a little lower beneath her. We were at least forty feet above the ground. The cows under us looked like miniature toys. I felt a bit like I did when I was in the basement, looking down at my tiny toy world. I looked up at the sky above her. It was dark and the clouds were gray. God's face had disappeared. When I looked back down, I joked, *"Should we jump?"*

I think I have early-onset dementia, or something. I hallucinate most when the sun goes down. Apparently, that's a symptom. I often feel withdrawn and chaotic. Those are symptoms too. I wrote before that I had an aortic aneurysm so it would be more cut-and-dried. I wanted to make it easier for you to get on the same page as me. I thought you'd be more likely to understand why I killed myself if I pretended to have some medical condition. I also thought it might be less upsetting to accept I died of a physical ailment than it would be to stomach that something was wrong with me mentally.

I don't know much about metaphors. I was terrible in English, but I remember Ms. Sweet explaining that in that confusing, "To be, or not to be" speech, Hamlet uses a mixed metaphor. He says, *Whether 'tis nobler in the mind to suffer / The slings and arrows of outrageous fortune, / Or to take arms against a sea of troubles, / And by opposing end them?*

To me, that's complete nonsense; however, my teacher said Hamlet was comparing his misfortunes to someone attacking him, and then to the sea. Those are metaphors, I think. He wasn't really talking about the sea or about being attacked. What he was talking about remains a mystery to me, but you get the point. It's symbolism.

In a metaphorical way, I did have an aneurysm, or cancer. I was stunted by symbolic tumors in my brain that made me hallucinate and feel hopeless. In a less Shakespearean way, however, I don't know what it was. I was seeing things. I was losing my grip on reality. It was getting worse every day.

I know that all of you would probably make a different choice if you were in my shoes. You might get specialists involved. You might ride it out. Move in with your parents. Live in a group home. That's why I lied. I wanted you to reach the same conclusion as me without having to understand why this is different for me.

I'm a different person than you are. I'm hesitant to spell that out because in similar situations in the past, I never successfully got that point across. I think people often judge others by their own standards. For example, some people who are gripped by weight loss and diet culture look at other people who eat high calorie foods and think, *Why would they eat like that? I would never eat like that. I have things figured out and they don't. Why don't they act like me?*

It doesn't occur to them that other people don't care about weight loss or diet, or that maybe they did in the past and overcame it. They don't realize that the people who aren't dieting might look at those who are and think, *Why would they eat like that? I would never eat like that. I have things figured out and they don't. Why don't they act like me?*

I think my mom didn't understand how I could be gay because she wasn't. Her lens on the world was different from mine. She viewed me being gay the way she would view herself being gay. The only reason she could come up with for why she would be is to get attention and bother people. She didn't grasp that someone could genuinely experience the world differently than her.

Queer people do it too sometimes. For example, the girl I was seeing often said, *"Everyone's a little gay,"* because she was bisexual, and that was her worldview.

I was not Margit. That's why I didn't finish high school. I don't think she understood that finishing high school was different for me than it was for her. She didn't realize that I was my own person, with my own identity, and had my reasons for why I did things, or didn't. I wasn't her.

Attempt Eighteen

I knew things were getting bad about six months ago. I found myself in that wooded area behind the cornfield near my parents' house. I don't remember how I got there. I was crouched in a muddy pile of dead leaves. The knees of my jeans were soaked. I had dug around a pine tree with my bare hands.

When I walked home, I was caked in dirt, and my fingers were so cold I couldn't bend them. Cars slowed down and rubbernecked as they passed me.

I scrubbed the dirt out from under my fingernails in my bathroom sink. I got mud all over the counter. I climbed into the shower and combed the earth out of my hair with my burning fingers. Black water pooled at my feet.

The summer before high school, I tried to run away from home. My parents were being swamp-monsters, Marg and I had gotten into a physical fight over a sweater, Grandma had recently been diagnosed with leukemia, and everything felt tense and stressful. I wanted to escape. I packed my backpack with two granola bars, a peach, Archie comic books, and my Barbie Jo.

I marched through my neighborhood, through the bare harvested cornfield, into that wooded area. I climbed inside the brush of a massive pine tree. I scaled its inner branches like a ladder. I perched as high as I could before the branches got weak. I sat there, high above the ground, like a bird.

I talked to Jo until the sun set. The two of us watched the sky turn orange through the pine needles, briefly red, and then black. It was late in the summer. It got chilly at dusk. I had eaten both granola bars and the peach. I wished I had packed more socks. I sucked on the peach pit, hungry, scrunching my frozen toes in my sneakers. I realized when it had gotten dark that I had to go back home.

It was around that moment I heard my family's voices in the distance. My dad's voice was the loudest—it boomed over everyone else's—but I could tell my whole family was there. I could hear Grandma's rickety old lady voice. Marg's weak little screech, and Mom and Jerry's frantic, similar yelps. They were all yelling my name.

I threw Jo and my backpack to the ground beneath the tree and started to climb down. I slipped on a few slick branches and almost fell. When my feet finally touched earth, I picked up my backpack and Jo. I remember her lips moving. She whispered that I had to leave her there. She said, *They'll know you ran away if they see you packed. You'll get in trouble. They'll put two and two together if I come with you. You have to leave me here with the backpack.*

I said, *"What? No. I don't want to do that."*

Her face stopped moving, and I held her plastic body like I would a dead bird.

My dad shouted my name again, panicked—like he was screaming the word "Fire!"

I dropped Jo on the ground and walked out of the pine trees
feeling traumatized. I stood in the clearing of the barren hayfield like
a baby who managed to toddle out of a house fire.

My mom spotted me and started sprinting in my direction. It
was so dark that everything looked like it was in black and white. I
had watched the sun set, so my eyes had adjusted. I could see Mom
like she was in some retro movie. She ran, her arms outstretched. She
shouted, "Oh my God. We were so worried!"

Everyone else rushed closely behind her. Dad said, *"Jesus Christ,
we almost called the cops. Where the hell were you?"*

I had never heard him say "Jesus Christ" or "hell" that way before. I
sensed as we all walked home that I was seeing everyone in a new light.
Mom told me she thought I was in the basement and went down to
find me for dinner, but couldn't. She searched the house, then called
Grandma and Jerry to check if I was with them. When she found out
that I wasn't, she started panicking. Dad and Marg drove around the
neighborhood searching for me. When the sun started setting, Jerry
and Grandma came over to help look for me. I think they were afraid
I had been abducted, or that I'd been hit by a van, or something.

"What were you doing?" Jerry asked.

"Playing," I said.

The word "playing" sounded strange then. I had used it so much
before, but it felt heavy in my mouth. I think that was the last time
I ever described myself "playing."

"Didn't you notice it got dark?" Grandma asked.

"It was too late," I said. *"It got dark before I noticed it did."*

———

The next morning, I returned to the woods to search for Jo. I hunted
around the base of the pine tree, but I couldn't find her. I thought

maybe I had the wrong tree. There were a lot of pine trees in those woods, and they all looked alike. I ended up searching for hours.

It was the end of summer. There were mounds of dead maple leaves covering the forest floor. I rummaged through them. I kept getting gross little white worms on my hands. The sun started to set. The sky was turning peach. I knew I couldn't keep looking.

A few days after, I accepted that Jo was lost forever. After stomaching that, I went down to the basement and broke all my Lego towers. I threw everything into Rubbermaid bins. Before returning upstairs, I looked around at the barren concrete. I stared at the pink walls. That day, I finally gave in to my desire to put my hands in the walls and squeeze. I felt prickly splinters slice the webs between my fingers. It felt like I was gripping a thousand flakes of grated glass.

After touching the walls, I went upstairs to sit in my bedroom with my sister and resolved to be more like she was. I wasn't a kid anymore. I was a teenager.

By September, I'd befriended Greta. We were spending every day together at school. She invited me to sleep over at her house. One Saturday night, we had eaten a pound of sour Skittles and watched back-to-back *Nightmare on Elm Street* movies. We were lying in her bed under a heavy quilt in the dark. Her window was ajar. The room was cold, and it smelled like wet leaves. I turned my head and asked her if she was asleep. She said, *"No, I'm still awake."*

She lived on the end of a street, at the edge of a forest. Her bedroom faced the trees. The air wafting in reminded me of being perched in that pine tree, sucking on my peach pit.

I told Greta about my pathetic attempt at running away and about losing Jo. I said I knew it was ridiculous, but it weighed on me. I told her I imagined birds ripping Jo's hair out to make their nests. I thought of her eyes being bleached by the sun. I thought of her lying under a tree, bald and faceless. Despite knowing rationally that she was a doll, she didn't matter, I still felt gutted by the whole thing. Almost every night, I found myself wincing into my pillow. Sometimes I woke up and gasped at the thought of Jo.

Greta and I had just become friends. We were good friends—we sat together in homeroom and we spent every lunch hour together—but still, we were *new* friends. I don't know what possessed me to tell her about Jo. If I had told Margit, or another friend, they would have laughed at me. They would have said I was immature and melodramatic. I risked humiliating myself telling Greta I was sad about my missing Barbie doll.

After I told her, I grimaced, realizing I might have embarrassed myself. I didn't want to wreck my new friendship with her. She was one of the only aspects of my life that I liked at the time. I went to school every day looking for her. Whenever the phone rang, I hoped it was her. When she invited me to sleep over that weekend, I tried on all my pajamas before packing. I felt sort of like I had a crush, but it wasn't a crush. I just felt intensely connected to her as a person. It would have devastated me if she started to dislike me, or if she thought I was weird for missing Jo.

I listened to the branches creak in the wind outside her window and braced myself for her to make fun of me. I felt cool air gust in on my face, and pictured myself lying in the woods, being buried under dead leaves, with no hair, my eyes and mouth bleached off.

Greta didn't make fun of me. She held my hand under the blankets.

I spent almost every weekend at Greta's for the rest of high school. Her mom joked that I was their other daughter. Her dad stocked this carbonated pink lemonade in their fridge because I liked it. I always drank it when I came over. Greta and I planned our class schedules to match. Whenever the phone rang, my family shouted, *"Is that Greta again?"*

I always had friends growing up, but this was different. I felt a sort of telepathy with her. When people spoke, we would exchange looks, and laugh sometimes without speaking.

I told her about how Marg and I called our parents swamp-monsters when they were angry. Whenever we had a bad teacher, or interacted with someone mean, Greta would mouth, *Swamp-monster,* at me. Eventually we joked that all of Drysdale was a bog, and that one day she and I would escape to someplace better.

In the twelfth grade, after Christmas, Greta's parents separated. Her dad immediately moved in with his new girlfriend. Greta talked about it coolly, like she didn't care. She joked that she had a new mommy. Because she joked about it, sometimes our friends would too. They'd tease, *"Do you think you'll get a new daddy, too?"* She laughed, but when she wasn't around, I told them to stop saying that. I knew the reason she joked about it was because treating it soberly set her off. It wasn't because she actually found it funny.

One night, a few months after her parents separated, she and I got drunk in the woods by her mom's place. She was sitting in the crotch of a big maple tree. Her head was leaned up against its trunk, and she was looking up at the branches above us. It was the beginning of spring. There were little buds growing on the tree's branches. She sighed and admitted she felt sad. She was facing the sky. I sat down next to her.

That night we pretended all the trees in the forest were sentient.

We named the maple tree Rodrigue. We pretended he was in an argument with Julie, the oak tree across from him.

Greta said, *"Rodrigue, please. Julie isn't having an affair."*

"She's immobile, Rodrigue."

"She is literally rooted in the ground."

———

There is this abandoned train bridge behind the hospital. It runs over the creek. It's high above the ground. It has these wooden slats with big gaps between them. Greta and I used to go there and run across the slats like fire walkers. Once, I tripped. I banged my shin and almost fell off the bridge. Greta helped me up while we laughed like lunatics. We could hardly breathe, we were laughing so hard. I wheezed, *"I almost died."*

When we got tired, we would sit on the bridge and swing our legs over the edge. Sometimes, we would throw rocks or hunks of wood down to watch them splash and form rings in the water.

I remember sitting on that bridge, looking down at our untied sneakers swinging above the water, chatting about our plans to move away. We considered becoming au pairs in Switzerland. Or going to school across the country. Or becoming garbage men in some big city. Buying a trailer, or a houseboat. Joining a fair. Riding boxcars. Starting a candy shop. We wanted to go somewhere fundamentally different from the hellmouth we were born in; somewhere we could spend our time occupied with something better than hurling rocks or hunks of wood off train bridges into creeks.

———

I went to the bridge with the girl I was seeing recently. I told her about how I used to run across it with a friend. She suggested we go and run too. We went there planning to play that game, but when we arrived, I saw dragonflies buzzing around the weeds beneath us.

It was as if someone died, the way I thought about Greta. This hollow, hopeless feeling would flare in my chest whenever I was reminded of her. She didn't escape Drysdale. She dug deeper into the bog, and got trapped there.

Rather than run across the bridge, I suggested we just sit and throw rocks and hunks of wood into the water.

Attempt Nineteen

I broke into that abandoned school on Alma Street with that girl I was seeing. We climbed in through a basement window like that raccoon did when I was a kid. She'd looked up the history of the building before we went. She told me it was built in the late 1800s. It was a liberal arts college for girls. It had been abandoned my whole life. It was dilapidated. The windows were shattered; people had thrown stones through them. The doors were boarded shut. She read its owners changed hands, went bankrupt, and then the college was deserted.

I had been inside the school before. There were limited things to do as a teenager in Drysdale. It was either loiter in a parking lot, amble around the mall, or sit inside Taco Bell. That abandoned school had a big draw. It was four stories high. It had turrets, and an arched tower in the center. I had gone there lots of times before with Greta.

It was twilight when I went with that girl. The school was dark inside. We brought a flashlight. I went in first and helped her through the window. The basement floor was covered in debris. There was broken wood and trash from people who had come before us.

She wanted to hook up in the basement. It smelled like beer and piss, though. I was worried someone else was inside.

We found the staircase. There were holes in the steps, and the railing was cracked and detached from the wall. We cautiously climbed up to the top, afraid with every step that we might plummet through the floor into the darkness. Once we reached the top story, she stood in the window in the center of the building. She looked out the cracked glass at Drysdale. She said, *"Imagine if this place caught fire. It would light right up."*

I faced the opposite way and pointed my flashlight on the wall behind us. I stared at the wall for a while. After admiring the view, she turned and asked me what I was looking at. I said, *"Nothing,"* but I was looking at graffiti. There was an old, spray-painted penis that Greta and I had painted there together.

About two months ago, I yelled at a Dollar Pal customer. She kept insisting that she needed to speak to a manager. At the time, we were being evacuated due to another bomb threat. She felt that was unacceptable. She was shouting. Everyone in the store gawked at us as they vacated. My coworker had tears in her eyes. I felt exhausted. I snapped. I said, *"What the fuck is wrong with you, lady?"*

She was stunned. She stepped backward. *"What? Why are you talking to me like that?"*

The lights in the store were so bright. I hadn't eaten all day. There was a homeless person sitting outside the store. They didn't move despite the bomb threat. They were strung out. Limp. Cops were picking them up. Manhandling them. The customer before her had to leave two cans of soup on the counter because they didn't have enough money to buy them. I was upset. Despite experiencing no recent injuries, I felt like I had been physically beaten. I felt like there were welts on my legs where I'd been kicked. I felt a goose egg budding on my skull, and my eyes swelling shut.

I started yelling, *"There's been a fucking bomb threat, lady! I can't help you! What do you want me to do? Stay here and scan your fucking Mr. Noodles while there's an active bomb threat? What is wrong with you?"*

She backed away from me like I was deranged. She started shouting for a manager.

I shouted back, *"I am the manager! Get the fuck out of my store!"* over and over until, finally, she evacuated.

Do you remember that time we went swimming in that pond near Grandma's house, Marg? It was shallow and the ground beneath the water was thick and mucky. When we stepped into it, our feet got suctioned, and we couldn't pull ourselves out. We had to scream for someone to come help us.

It took a while for anyone to come. While we shouted, I remember imagining us being pulled under the water, beneath the slimy muck. I pictured us being entombed in that mud for a season, until we emerged like frogs do after they hibernate, or until we suffocated and died.

Would you rather become a frog or suffocate to death?

Marg, when we were kids, and our parents were being swamp-monsters, did you ever see tentacles growing out of their heads?

When Dad punched that hole in our bedroom wall, and his fist emerged from the plaster, did you see scales on his knuckles?

At Christmas, when Mom kept saying the R-word, did her hair look greasy, wet, and green? At Thanksgiving, when Dad said something racist, did it look like all his teeth fell out, and like his entire body was coated in this oily green slime? Did anyone else see that?

I thought everyone at that table looked slimy. When I went home and I looked in the mirror, I looked greasy too. Did you notice that? Did you ever see tentacles growing out of my head?

Attempt Twenty

I had a stuffed unicorn who liked eating grass in meadows and carrying other toys on her back. Jo would ride her around the basement. The two would talk about flowers and about the human foods that horses could eat, like peppermints and sunflower seeds.

I had a group of Polly Pockets named Mallory, Ainsley, and Corrina. They lived in a little purple heart-shaped house with a pink bed and a stone fireplace in it. I played that they were cobbler elves who snuck around the basement at night, helping the other toys with their chores, fixing the broken parts of the world while everyone else was snoozing.

I planned birthday parties for my toys.

I played that they had magic powers.

I played that they built castles.

They had dances.

They baked cakes.
They brewed potions.

When I grew up, I realized I could never be a unicorn or a cobbler elf. I could never be a troll, an old man, an astronaut, a shark, or a rat. I would never be a girl who everyone liked. Those weren't options for me. I was assigned the person I am. I had no choice. Even if I got extreme plastic surgery, covered myself in tattoos, buzzed all my hair off, amputated a leg, or gained or lost a hundred pounds—there were parts of me I could never change. I was assembled with the bones I came with.

I used to listen to music zealously. I used to sing along, impassioned by lyrics I didn't relate to because I imagined someday I might. I could picture being the person singing. I could feel my feet in their shoes. When I got older and heard music I didn't relate to, I shut it off.

I don't relate to big, inspirational songs about overcoming obstacles, or being a hero. Bright songs that reflect some happy party life sound totally alien to me. I won't ever relate to songs about feeling huge, crushing love. I'm a lesbian in a small town. I can't meet anyone new. I don't have enough life in me to resonate with tragic ballads about revenge or breakups. I can't listen to songs about places I'll never go to. I don't connect with any of them.

It's not that I was desperate to be someone else. It's not that I hated myself. It's just that when you get older, you are suddenly required to be the person you are. I felt like I was cast as a character I wasn't able to play. Maybe in a different setting, in a different production, with a different cast—I might have pulled it off. In Drysdale, in the play I was cast in, it wasn't the part for me.

This isn't some miserable, self-loathing thing, it's just that I don't want this. I could handle being a broke high-school dropout, trapped in a conservative small town, surrounded by people who I find, and who find me, insufferable. I would have gritted my teeth and played myself. I could not, however, play that character and also be insane and all alone. It's not the part for me. I felt like my dress rehearsal had ended, and I had grown up. I was cracked by the trauma of losing my friend, I felt isolated and resentful, and I couldn't picture any future for myself.

If I could have picked what I was born to be, I would be a fat little rat at a fair. I would ride the Ferris wheel all night. All the carnival lights would reflect in my happy, beady eyes. I would feast on candy apple cores, discarded peanuts, and melon rinds. I would spook ladies and carnival workers for kicks. When the lights went out, and the gates were shut, I would scurry around on the ground, rummage through trash cans, and squeak happily with my rat pals. I would live to be about two years old, which is as long as most rats live. I would get my money's worth out of my little rat lifespan, and I would leave the earth happy to have been there.

I didn't want to say this because it sounds crazy, but at family dinners, I saw a literal elephant in the room. He was this enormous, deranged elephant. His tusks were covered in blood, and his eyes were all white. He was always huffing at me. I knew I couldn't mention him, so I pretended not to notice him. I said, *"Hey Dad, can you pass the sweet-potato casserole?"* while the elephant stomped his feet and threatened to crush me.

I listened to my family chatter while out of the corner of my eye I watched the elephant pant. Sometimes some of you asked why I seemed so distracted. Jerry often said I seemed "far away."

"It's impolite to be so disengaged," Marg always said.

Whenever I entered the house, I was afraid of that giant elephant. I was worried I would slip up, mention him, and freak you all out. At Christmas, it seemed like everyone else saw him too. I thought I saw Dad feeding him. Did you see him? Were we all pretending we didn't see him? Were you in on something I wasn't?

<hr>

I felt on edge. Sometimes I thought I heard the girl I was seeing whispering things on her phone. I heard her hushing things like, *"It's dangerous. You better get out."*

<hr>

I lied earlier when I said I had no hard feelings toward any of you. I wanted to pretend I didn't because I had to kill myself, and I didn't want you all to feel bad about that. The truth is, I did have hard feelings toward you. I don't want to guilt-trip you about that now, and I'm not saying it because I want you to feel bad. I really don't want you to feel bad. If I could choose, no one would ever feel bad. I wouldn't even want that deranged elephant to feel bad. I wish he could be taken to live in the savannas, or wherever elephants are supposed to live.

<hr>

A few weeks ago, Greta's mug shot was posted on Drysdale's community Facebook page. She didn't look like herself. Her lips were cracked. She had this far-off expression. People commented. They wrote things like,

Trash and Why is she still allowed to live here? One person wrote a lengthy comment about an encounter they had with her. They spotted her wandering topless on Main Street. They pulled over and tried to give her a coat. She refused to take it. They insisted, and she hit them. I think maybe they tried to force the coat on her, or maybe she was scared of them for some reason.

They wrote that they had to call the cops on her. Greta was taken in for both assault and indecent exposure. Their comment got over a hundred likes. People replied:

> You are so kind for trying, but people like her are beyond help.

> This type of person is dangerous. the town needs to do something to get them out of here.

> This is why we need to vote for kevin fliner.

I told the girl I was seeing about Greta. I told her how she and I were best friends, and how alone I felt without her. I felt sick about it. I couldn't sleep. I cried, telling her about how she used to be. I told her I hated this town. I said, *"This place is a cesspool."* I hated that no one was doing anything to help. Why wasn't anyone doing anything? Why would they vote for this guy who would make it even worse? He wanted to close the safer supply services and supervised consumption sites in our clinics and community centers. He was going to kill her. I was so afraid to hear she was dead. I told the girl I was seeing that I blamed myself for Greta. I was beside myself.

She told me it wasn't my fault, and that she wanted to get revenge for Greta.

I said, *"What do you mean, revenge?"*

She said, *"Don't worry about it."*

I said, *"Wait, what do you mean?"*

She said, *"I am going to fuck shit up. I'm going to scare people."*
I was out of my mind by this point. I was seeing things.

She whispered, while tentacles grew out of her temples, *"Did you know Kevin Fliner's campaign office is in the building next to the Dollar Pal?"*

Attempt Twenty-One

I made this more complicated than it had to be, didn't I? I should have just written the truth and left it at that. I got bogged down thinking, *How can I avoid upsetting people?* I thought maybe if I said I was sick, you would all understand. If I said I was crazy, you might get it.

I wasn't really crazy. Well, maybe I was. I wasn't seeing things that weren't there, at least. There was no moving turtle in a poster. I didn't see a deranged elephant, God's face in the sky, or tentacles growing out of anyone's head. I made that up. It was symbolism, I think. I don't know. I was playing.

I can't play like that anymore, can I?

The truth is I had an opioid addiction too. I didn't want to reveal that because I knew it would disappoint you. I lied earlier when I said I tried it once. I tried it all the time.

No. I'm sorry. I'm pretending again. I didn't really have an opioid problem. I joined a cult. We drank this toxic Kool-Aid because some guy in a bathrobe told us if we did, we would get to live forever in another dimension.

I wouldn't want to live forever, would you?

Sorry. Okay. The actual truth is I'm running away. I'm faking my death. Don't try to find me. I joined the circus. I've moved some-place tropical.

No, I can't do that, can I?

I have to grow up.

I wish the internet didn't exist. I wish I could be like a deadbeat dad in the fifties and start a new family a couple cities over or hop in a boxcar and move undetected across the country. I wish I could move to Europe, take on a new name, or pretend I had amnesia.

When I went on that trip to France, I wanted to stay there. That was my harebrained intention. I wanted to book a one-way ticket, but you can't just fly to France and live there. That's not how things really work. You have to do paperwork. You need a visa, or some-thing. Besides, France wouldn't want me. I didn't even graduate high school. There was no way, really, for me to run away.

It would have been nice if I could have run away, wouldn't it? I would have done that, if I could have, I think.

I was so worried about Greta. It was this constant weight on me. I felt like I was watching her die in slow motion. I wanted to snap her out of it. Shake her awake.

When we were teenagers, I thought she and I were in cocoons, or chrysalises, or whatever the right word is. I figured we were in that mucky stage between being caterpillars and butterflies. I thought one day we would solidify and emerge from our casings with bright orange, pink, and white wings. We would migrate like butterflies do, to the Tropic of Cancer, or wherever they go.

When we hatched, we were these little white moths, destined for nothing greater than chewing through wool sweaters. I realized then that I couldn't be anything I wanted. I understood that if I mustered every ounce of my will, Greta would still be lost. I comprehended, finally, that life doesn't work the way I thought it would, and that I had no control over that.

Greta's mom called me to tell me Greta had stolen jewelry from her aunt and taken her grandpa's credit card. She had stolen cash from her father and her stepmom. She'd taken bikes and tools out of their neighbor's garage. She warned me to lock my doors and not to trust her. She said Greta needed help. I already knew she needed help, but hearing it from her mom felt like hearing it from God's voice booming in the sky.

At the time, I felt like Greta and I were riding on these rafts. I felt like we had escaped a shipwreck and we were paddling to shore, but we drifted. A haphazard wind coasted her so far away that I couldn't reach her, but I could still see her. I had to watch her float out into the horizon.

I wondered if we could still bring her back. I asked her mom. I thought maybe with her parents involved, we could make her see somehow. I asked her what we could do, and she started crying. She said, *"I don't know. I'm not sure there's anything we can do. I've been trying. Her dad's been trying. I know you've been trying too."*

Sometimes I think teenagers are viewed as dramatic and emotional because their souls are trying to rattle out of their bodies while they morph into swamp-monsters. Sometimes I think adults all feel just as intensely as teenagers do, but they're restrained inside their monster bodies. There were times when I looked into adults' eyes, like my mom's, or Jerry's, or Greta's parents', and I thought I saw something inside them rattling chains. Before I died, there were times I thought I saw it in my own eyes in the mirror.

I remember smacking firecrackers at squirrels and catching snowflakes on my tongue. I've held my head out car windows in the summer and cupped fireflies in my palms. I used to spend hours by myself with my dolls, making up happy stories, believing I was capable of growing wings.

I'm not sure there is a way to be alive without upsetting people. We're all in this web together, aren't we? Everything we do tangles everybody else together.

Inaction is an action. I realized that when I didn't submit my *Hamlet* paper. When I didn't stop Greta from making bad choices. Not doing something is doing something.

When Grandma dug up her garden and she found that big dead dog, she rushed inside the house to scrub her hands and cry. Marg hollered at me not to, but I looked inside the hole. I saw the bones in the dirt. They must have been underground for a while. There was no flesh left. I picked up the skull of the dog with my bare hands. I held it and looked into its empty eye sockets, and at its long, pointed fangs.

Do you think the right thing to do is to live out your life, even when you feel like you're becoming a swamp-monster? Should I have stayed alive, been a grown-up, and tried to fix things? Do you think the reason most people with bad lives don't kill themselves is just because they're afraid of dying? Is that really it? I think dying is less scary than growing up. I'd rather die than grow up to be a shitty person.

I wonder what dying feels like. Do you think it feels like sleeping? I guess sometimes we dream when we're sleeping. We have nightmares. Do you think death might feel like that? Is that what's keeping people alive?

I'm not sure if any of that matters to me. I don't care if dying is like sleeping. I don't think that is really the question at all.

The
Truth

One

I don't think anyone is going to read this. I don't know why I'm still writing it. I'm not achieving what I set out to do. I think I'm just trying to make sense of it all, but it's a mess. None of it makes sense. Sigrid's on life support. She has a feeding tube. I'm sitting beside her. Every time I look up, I expect to see her eyes open, but they haven't. She asked me to come. I drove forty minutes, thinking she wanted to talk in person. We argued at Christmas, and I thought maybe she wanted to reconcile. I found a folded piece of paper taped to her door. On the front it said, *Don't come in, I'm dead,* and inside it said, *Can you write this for me, Marg?*

I tried to come up with some reason that would be better than nothing. I thought maybe cancer or an impending aneurysm would be best. I thought Dad could get on board with that, but then I realized everyone would see through those lies immediately. I didn't think it through.

I read Sigrid's diary. I read it to try to understand why she did this, and to try to write this in her voice. Writing it felt the way I imagine she felt when she was holding one of her dolls. I felt like I was in the basement, holding my sister. I knew I couldn't sound exactly like her, so I tried to be manipulative by writing that she'd asked me to edit this. Anyone reading who suspected the note sounded like me could think it was because I edited it.

I feel like I'm in a nightmare. I thought she was going to wake up. I thought I was just busying myself writing this. I thought everything would be okay, and I could erase everything. I felt like I was preparing for the worst-case scenario—one I didn't actually expect to happen. I thought ultimately, she would read whatever I drafted, we would find some dark humor in it, and I could say, *Fuck you for that*. She would say, *Sorry, I don't know what I was thinking*, and then she would live to be one hundred and two. The first time I came to the hospital, I brought coffee for her. I thought she would wake up.

I don't know what I'm doing. Why am I writing this? I can't believe she hasn't woken up. It's been five days, and this stupid note is so long now.

Is this actually happening? Am I dreaming? Every day I wake up and gasp at my reality. There's this second before I'm fully lucid when I'm not thinking about it, but then I remember, and it knocks the wind out of me. I don't know what to do. I keep writing. I'm sitting beside her, watching her chest go up and down, and I'm writing this asinine note to distract myself because she asked me to.

I don't think I've faced that this is actually happening. Is this really happening? I've been occupying my mind with this note as if it's a writing assignment. I'm afraid the second I stop writing, I'll have to confront this hideous reality, and I'd rather explode.

I can't imagine anything that would devastate me more than Sigrid dying. This is the worst thing that could ever happen to me. It's like someone ran me over. Did someone run me over? I feel crushed. I could leave this hospital room and find every other human on earth decapitated, and I would be less disturbed than I am by this. I feel eviscerated.

I don't think I'm even fully facing this. What's going to happen when I really face this? I think I'll die.

Am I insane? Is this really happening?

I need to wake up.

I'm pinching my arm.

I'm pulling my hair.

I just screamed "Wake up!" at her. I did it right into her ear. The little hairs by her ear moved from the gust of my scream.

Oh my God. This is really happening. My sister tried to kill herself, and she isn't waking up.

A nurse came into the room. She heard me shout. She asked me if everything was okay, and I said yes.

Why did I say yes?

I'm so mad at you, Sigrid. I feel like I am a thousand angry swamp-men. I would rather you had murdered me than this. I would rather you had intentionally run me over with a car for no reason. I would rather you had backed up and run me over, over and over. This is the worst thing you could ever have done to me. I feel torn in half.

How could you ask me to write this? How could you ask me to come? That was a terrible thing to do to me. Fuck you.

At first I was just going to write, "Sorry," but that felt so sad. I imagined Mom reading that and feeling crushed, so I tried to write more. I tried to write it so that someone reading might feel less upset. I thought that's what you would want. Is it? I don't know.

I read everything I could find in your apartment. I read your receipts. Your junk mail. I looked through all your papers. I found all of your *Hamlet* essay drafts. They were good, I thought, Sigrid. I think you would have passed if you had handed one in.

I wish you had written this. What would you say? Would you have written more about topics I couldn't, like periods and politics? I think you would have. I should have made this whole thing ruder. How would you have written me?

Don't come in, I'm dead . . . Can you write this for me, Marg?

That's what you wrote me. That's the reality. That is the message I got.

I can't write this for you. I can't do it.

I stopped trying to make this note make people feel better, and started trying to understand why you did this. I realized while reading some of your journal entries about me that I was domineering. I was constantly nudging your ribs, trying to control everyone's feelings. I wish I hadn't done that. I'm sorry.

Can you wake up and forgive me?

We hardly played together when we were kids because you were so particular about your toys. You never played and imagined storylines that were sad or fueled by conflict. I usually pretended our dolls were fighting, and you would frown. You would say, *"That's not how I want to play."*

You wrote a lot of diary entries. You wrote about Greta and Kevin. You wrote about how you and I fought when we were kids. Then your entries got shorter. In the last month, you wrote nothing.

I should erase this, shouldn't I? I should just write, *I love you and I'm sorry.* That doesn't sound like you, and it makes me feel sick, but maybe that's okay. Maybe that's what Mom and Dad would want to read. I think it's what Jerry would want.

I copied parts of your diary directly into this note. I was trying to sound exactly like you. I toiled over this the way I toil over school assignments. I made notes of the vocabulary you used. I repeated words you repeated. I read your emails and texts. I copied how you phrased things. I read my attempts, over and over. There were times when I thought, *I've done a good job. This sounds like her.*

That's sick, isn't it? Why am I still writing? I don't know what's driving me to do this. I'm not getting a grade. I don't get a degree at the end of forging a believable suicide note. What's wrong with me?

I'm sorry I read all your private thoughts in your diary. I'm sorry I went through your phone, your email, and your things. I'm sorry you were feeling the way you were, and that I didn't help you. I'm sorry that my instinct is to soften this, or to cover it up somehow, rather than to do whatever normal people do.

What do normal people do?

There is something wrong with me. I don't react to my sister attempting to kill herself by crying or calling my mom. Instead, I squash how I feel into a pit in my stomach and use that to fuel springing into action. I hyperfocus on whatever I can do to make it better.

I want to control things. That's why I undertook this. I felt like it was the only thing I could control. I wanted to direct how Mom, Dad, and Jerry would react to this. I wanted to force everyone to feel better. *I* wanted to feel better. I didn't want to face that this was happening. I wanted to occupy myself with this stupid assignment so I could feel accomplished. I thought that might take the edge off.

There is nothing I can do to make this better.

Maybe I should write, "It's your fault!" because you'd find that funny, wouldn't you? What you find funny doesn't always overlap with what others find funny, though. The risk is high that people would read it and actually think this was their fault.

Is this my fault?

This should be short. This is way too long. I always write too much when I'm confused. I ramble on and on, thinking I can make sense of things if I just write enough. I handed in a paper a month ago that was way over the page count because I didn't understand the readings.

You always acted like I was so smart and had everything figured out, but I didn't. I thought you did.

Every word means more when there are fewer of them. Brevity is the soul of wit, or whatever. If I were able to pick just the right words for this, it would be brief. I have to add more words to make the words I've already written mean less.

There is no good way to write this. There is nothing I could write that would make anyone feel better.

I don't want to leave you in the woods, Sigrid. I don't want your hair to be used in bird nests or for your face to fade in the sun. I want you to wake up and eat a hot dog at a fair.

I'm watching you right now. You look pale. Maybe I should crawl under your bed and kick your mattress like you did to me in our bunk beds.

I wish I didn't care so much about upsetting people.

If you die, I'll never recover.

If you die, I'm going to die.

Sigrid, it *was* soppy that time I prayed for you. I say, "I pray for my sister," every night now. Even before this happened. I've done it ever since I moved out. I did it in my dorm. I'll do it until I'm an old lady. Even if I stop believing in God, every single night I'm going to say, "I pray for my sister." Those are going to be my dying words.

Please wake up.

Two

I love you and I'm sorry.

Three

There was an accident on the highway. It took me forever to get home. Cops and ambulances took over half the road. Cars were crawling in one lane, rubbernecking. A pickup truck was upside down in the ditch. There didn't seem to be another vehicle involved. I think maybe the driver nodded off or swerved for an animal.

I once involuntarily swerved for a jaywalking raccoon. The raccoon stood up on its hind legs, stunned by my headlights. I remember his masked, reflective eyes. He was holding one of his small, humanlike paws to his chest. He looked dazed. I veered away from him and almost rammed into a barricade.

It must be strange to come upon a highway when you're a woodland creature. When there are woods on either side of a road, that road is inside a forest. It doesn't feel that way when you're driving, but if we were birds looking down, it would be clear that trees were cut down to pave a street. Geographically and ecologically, the habitat that the road is in is a forest. When raccoons or deer turn into roadkill, it's not because they went somewhere they shouldn't have. It's because there was an unnatural street in their woods.

When I almost hit that raccoon, I didn't drive into a barricade or a ditch. I screamed, swerved, and then veered back. Maybe in another universe I rolled my car or drove into a tree. I wouldn't be shocked to learn there is a reality where I died to spare a portly little forest creature.

———————

I was hoping to sneak inside my apartment. I live with friends I made in first year. I didn't want to cross paths with anyone, but my roommates were in the front room. I could hear them through the door. I hesitated in the hallway before entering. I stood with my keys in my hand.

I cried driving home. My vision was blurred by tears. I gripped my steering wheel and sat forward the way old people do, hoping that being a few inches closer to my windshield would negate my hazy vision. My throat had this raw lump in it. I was sobbing in a way I only can in the privacy of a car alone at night.

I could tell my face was flushed and swollen. My eyes felt puffy and red. I inhaled, withheld tears, and waited until enough time passed to believably blame my appearance on allergies. There was snow on the ground. It looked like icing.

I decided to pretend I'd been around a long-haired cat. I'm not allergic to cats, but I think the trick to lying is to convince yourself. If you believe it, other people will too.

I am allergic to long-haired cats.

I was in Drysdale all week. I didn't tell my friends or my roommates I was going, or why. They texted our group chat daily, Where are you, marg? I lied and said I was at a friend's place. They replied,

Which friend?

Someone we don't know?

I want to meet this friend.

When I finally mustered the courage to walk inside my apartment, I found my roommates sitting with some of our neighbors. We live in a fourplex, and we've befriended the girls next door, and the couple who live above them. When I entered the room, they all looked up.

Candace smiled. "There she is!"

Sadiyah said, "Our missing girl!"

They were drinking red wine and playing Settlers of Catan.

Fatma, our neighbor, immediately noticed my inflamed face. She asked if I was okay.

I said, "I am allergic to long-haired cats."

Joe frowned. "You are?"

Candace asked whose house I was staying at.

I said, "It's a secret."

I could sense they were all confused, but I didn't want to deal with telling them the truth. I don't know how they'd react. There isn't a reaction they could give that I would want. I don't want them to feel sorry for me, feel uncomfortable, or sad. I don't want to have to navigate my friendships under the weight of all this. I would rather never talk about it.

They invited me to have a drink and play with them. They said they would start the game over so I could join, but I declined. I said, "Thanks, but I'm too tired. I'm just going to hit the hay."

I would like a drink, but I'm glad I didn't accept one. I say things I regret when I drink. I morph into this strange version of myself. I gripe about the stress of my student loans and my classes. I bemoan my childhood; I talk about how angry my parents were, and how my sister was a loose cannon. I cry about ex-boyfriends and guys who have been mean to me. I talk about how I have no money, and how I hate all my clothes. I unload on my friends in ways I would never dream of sober. I have sobbed in bar bathrooms and in the back seat of more than one cab. I have flashes of this mortifying memory where I'm sitting on a curb. It's three a.m. My makeup is smudged on the cuffs of my shirt. My friends are surrounding me, and I can hear myself weeping. I'm ruining their night.

When I'm sober, I'm careful not to overshare. I listen more than I speak. I ask people how they are, and when they ask me back, I say, "I'm great, thank you."

After I drink, I wake up cringing, regretting how I burdened everyone around me with all my petty sorrows. I can't imagine the remorse I would feel if I woke up after burdening people with sorrows that weren't trivial.

I couldn't sleep. I kept waking up, gasping. I could hear everyone outside my door. They were laughing. I could hear the couple who live in the unit above my bedroom. I have never met them, but I often hear them. The floor is thin. They were fighting. The man was yelling. I couldn't make out what he was saying. His voice was muffled, but he sounded mad.

They argue a lot. The sound of them fighting often confuses me in my sleep. I wake up thinking I'm in my childhood bedroom with Sigrid, and it's our parents fighting. Despite the fact that being in the vicinity of an argument ignites my fight-or-flight response, I have this instinct to whisper, *It's okay, Sigrid*, before I open my eyes.

I wanted to sleep. I'd spent the last five days sleeping upright in a stiff hospital chair. I felt delirious. Every time I drifted off, I was startled awake by the angry man upstairs, my friends outside laughing, or by my own dreaded thoughts.

I missed all my classes last week. All my midterms are coming up. I was already falling behind before last week, but now it's gotten dire.

I wish I could just focus on what I need to do. I wish there were some way to click everything off except the part of me that studies and keeps myself alive. I don't want to think about anything but sleeping, eating, reading, and going back to sleep.

I arrived five minutes late to class this morning. I sat in the back of the room. I felt like I had a fever. I was sweating but still felt cold. There was this strange ache in my legs. I was sipping coffee despite feeling jittery, and my hands were trembling. I kept splattering drops of the coffee from its lid in scalding dots on my hands. There were little red burn marks on my skin. It looked like I had a pox.

My professor was talking about *Anna Karenina*. I have not kept up with the readings. I don't know what the book is about. Based on today's lecture, I think it's about adultery, but I'm not sure. I only half listened.

I was watching a bird outside the window. It was a red bird. It wasn't bright red. It was a dull, brownish burgundy. I wondered how old it was. I wondered how old it would live to be. I doubt wild birds live long. Three years, maybe.

I was called on to answer a question. I didn't register the question, but I knew I wouldn't know the answer regardless of it being repeated, so I apologized and confessed, "I don't know."

My professor shook his head, disappointed. The class isn't very big. I'm sure he noticed I was absent last week. He probably thinks I'm a bad student. Maybe *I am* a bad student.

College is bizarre. These scholarly, cerebral professors are surrounded by ignorant, hungover young people. I guess that's the point, but it's an odd crowd to be in. It's strange for an old man to speak for hours in front of an audience of disinterested youth on Adderall. It makes me feel like everything is fake. It makes me feel like I am in another dimension.

At the end of today's lecture, my friend Shannon offered to send me her notes from last week. I thanked her, and she said, "No problem. You look terrible. Is everything okay?"

I told her I felt drained but that I was fine, and I thanked her again for her notes.

———

The *Anna Karenina* audiobook is thirty-seven hours long. I went to the library between classes, put my headphones on, and listened to a robotic narrator speed through one hour of the story on fast-forward. I was weaving in and out of awareness. I was not following the story.

There were strangers sitting at my table with me. One of them had his elbows on the table and his hands in his hair. He looked stressed. I wondered what he was studying. I thought of asking him but decided not to. I didn't want to bother him.

———

Sometimes I suspect everything that has happened since I was eight years old has been a dream. I think maybe I'll wake up tomorrow, in the top bunk close to the ceiling, under my childhood quilt. I'll wrestle Sigrid for the bathroom, brush my teeth with sparkle toothpaste, and ride a yellow bus to school. The seats will have torn faux leather with exposed orange foam innards. I'll wear my clear, plastic raincoat. I can even smell that synthetic vinyl material.

If I woke up tomorrow and I was eight again, it wouldn't faze me. In fact, I might feel less disturbed to wake up as myself at eight than I would to wake up and be me at twenty-one.

Am I really twenty-one? I'm in my third year of school, but I feel like I'm a kid.

I remember looking at the multicolored alphabet border surrounding my elementary school library like it was yesterday. There was a bulletin board with anthropomorphic book worms waving at me. I remember sitting crisscross applesauce on a carpet that looked like a clock before a wooden rocking chair, while a kindly old librarian read me *Where the Wild Things Are*. I remember bookshelves full of bright picture books, and literary-themed stuffed animals like Winnie the Pooh and Franklin the Turtle.

The library here feels sterile. There are no multicolored borders or rocking chairs. There are just big wooden tables and rows of plain, boring, legal books. There isn't even art on the walls. It feels like something is missing. It all feels very fake.

Am I eight years old, dreaming that I'm in college? Does the library feel empty because I'm small and ignorant and I don't know what to dream up?

I tried to hang out with my roommates earlier to appear normal. I didn't want them to think something was off with me. We were standing in the kitchen. They were talking about whether God exists. Sadiyah is studying philosophy. She has a midterm tomorrow morning. Her study notes say, in bold red letters: *GOD IS DEAD*.

I tuned out while they discussed Aristotle. I stared at the oranges on our counter. I wondered if they were ripe. I'm awful at selecting fruit. I can't tell if it's rotten from the outside. When I'm grocery shopping, I knock on watermelons and grip tangerines as if I know something about assessing fruit, but I don't. I feel like I don't know the things I'm supposed to. I feel like I'm pretending.

After staring at the oranges too long, I started to feel like crying. I told Sadiyah and Candace I felt tired, and retreated to my bedroom.

Hours later, there was a knock on my door. I opened it and found a plate of sliced oranges on the floor waiting for me. Sadiyah put it there. She always cuts up fruit for us.

If God doesn't exist, I wonder if reincarnation does. If it does, I wonder if we are reborn again and again forever, or if we are reborn a certain number of times, and then expire. If that's the case, I think I'm on my last life. I have this deep sense that I am extremely old. Sometimes, I feel like I can remember being someone I'm not. Places I've never been before feel familiar. Foods I've never eaten taste like something I've tasted before.

I just called Sigrid's hospital room. In tears, I asked, "Are you alive?"

She answered, "Do you have my phone?"

I repeated, "I don't remember. Are you alive?"

She said, "Obviously I'm alive. You keep calling me to ask that, and I keep asking you where my phone is. What do you mean you don't remember? Where is my phone?"

I don't remember calling her. Apparently, I've been calling her a lot.

Today I wore a sweater I don't remember buying. It's a black knit. I wouldn't have bought it before university because it's the kind of sweater Sigrid would have stolen from me. When I lived in Drysdale, I avoided buying clothes I worried Sigrid might take. We were different sizes and had different styles, but she would steal my plain sweaters and T-shirts. I didn't like sharing with her. She wasn't careful with her stuff. She got stains on her clothes. She lost things.

In high school, I bought all my clothes with the money I made working part-time at the laundromat. My parents stopped buying me clothes when I was a teenager because they couldn't afford to get me things I wanted, and I felt embarrassed wearing the clothes they *could* offer me. I saved my own money to buy my clothes, so I had the good sense to take care of them. When Sigrid wore anything of mine, I freaked out.

I don't remember thinking about Sigrid when I bought the black knit sweater I wore today. I used to choose clothes by their fit, price, fabric quality, and risk of being stolen by her. A plain black sweater would have been exactly what Sig would swipe. I wouldn't have bought it. Somewhere along the line, I stopped considering that. We didn't live in the same house. We didn't share a closet. I didn't have to worry about her.

This all occurred to me when I took off my sweater today. I looked at it and realized something had changed without me noticing it. This disturbed me. I took all my clothes out of my closet and dresser, threw them on the floor of my room, and examined them. I made a pile of everything I thought Sigrid might steal. In the last three years, I have amassed several items she would have taken from me. Crew neck sweaters. White cotton tees. I can't recall when I stopped thinking about her.

I spent over an hour crying, hugging my crew necks and T-shirts on the floor of my bedroom. I had makeup on. I got foundation and mascara marks all over my things. I was rubbing my face in the fabric.

My grandma died of blood cancer over two years ago now. She was old, but it still knocked the wind out of me. We knew she had cancer for years. I knew it was coming, but somehow, it still took me by surprise.

I'd never experienced someone close to me dying before. I thought I knew what it would be like, but I didn't.

I'd considered Grandma to be an immediate family member. She was always at our house. Sigrid and I spent a lot of time in her garden. We could go to her place and walk inside without knocking. We felt comfortable opening her fridge. Eating her food. Taking a nap on her couch. Running a bath.

I was surprised by some of my feelings when she died. I knew I'd feel devastated, and I did, but there were other feelings I didn't expect. One thing I really wrestled with was feeling like there was less love in the world for me. When she died, I felt a shift in the universe. It was more than her absence. I felt the cosmic void where her love for me used to be, like an empty stomach after puking. On top of feeling shattered by her absence, I felt less important with her gone, and also guilty for feeling that way. I wasn't just mourning her life. I was mourning her love for me. When she died, I felt selfishly less important, and every time I lose someone, I'll have less purpose. I will degrade in value the longer I live, until there is no point to me.

I called Sigrid earlier to ask, "Are you alive?"

She said, "Yes, do you have my phone?"

I forgot she asked me to bring her phone.

"You're alive, for sure?" I clarified.

She said, "You keep asking me that. I'm alive, okay? Listen. I'm talking. How could I talk if I were dead? What's going on? Can you bring me my phone? Are you insane?"

I have this sense that there is a world where Sigrid died, and I forget if I am living in that universe, or not. Even when she talks to me on the phone, I wonder if I've caught her in an alternate reality. I wonder if cosmic wires crossed, and if my version of her is really on the line with me, or not.

I sense that in some way it isn't really her. I feel this shadowy, lingering grief that she is dead. Maybe I'm sensing the intensity of my grief in another timeline. Maybe she died somewhere else. Or maybe I'm insane.

"Are you in the same universe as me?"

I called her again.

"What are you talking about?"

"Am I talking to the version of you who I know? Like, did we grow up together?"

"Marg, I'm literally in a psych ward right now, and you're freaking *me* out. Do you have my phone or not? I think you've lost it."

"Lost what?" I ask.

I do feel like I lost something.

Four

Mo texted me.

Are we still friends?

He and I aren't really friends. We make out at parties. He texts me good morning every day. He likes everything I post on social media, and whenever my friends run into him, they come back and tell me, "Mo has a crush on you."

I haven't replied to him in over a week because I've been so preoccupied. He must think something is wrong. He must think I don't like him anymore.

I replied,

Yes, i'm sorry. I've just been really busy.

He texted back,

I was worried about you. is everything okay?

I didn't reply.

The man who lives above me had another temper tantrum last night. He stomped around like an enraged baby elephant. I think he wears steel-toe boots or tap shoes. His girlfriend was shouting his name, which is either Dan or Stan. She was crying, "*Stop it, Dan* (or Stan). *I love you!*"

I don't know if my roommates or my neighbors hear them. No one has ever mentioned how often they fight before. We have discussed that the woman seems shy, and the man seems standoffish. They never say hello to any of us, and all the other people in the building are friends.

They've been screaming all year. It's gotten more frequent lately, but I've been hearing it since we moved in. Maybe my bedroom is positioned beneath theirs. Maybe I bear the brunt of it.

My eyes felt like raisins this morning. I sat at the back of the classroom. The prof wrote on the board, *Why did Anna kill herself?*

I didn't know that Anna killed herself. I hadn't reached that part of the book.

The prof erased the line, and rewrote, *Why does Anna regret killing herself?*

I thought that was an interesting question. I wondered, *Is there an afterlife in* Anna Karenina? *How would we know she regrets it if she's dead? Maybe she doesn't die. That would be nice.*

A student answered, "Anna mistakenly believes that killing herself is the only escape from her infelicitous life. It doesn't dawn on her, until it's too late, that she's made an error."

"Infelicitous" is an odd word to use, isn't it? I've never heard someone say "infelicitous" so offhandedly like that. Why do people speak like that in college? They're always doing that. They insert words that feel weird and clunky into their sentences.

Another student said, "Let's be more direct about why. It's because of the author's politics. What kind of message would Tolstoy be leaving us with if it ended in her killing herself, and no notes about why that's bad?"

I wasn't following. Later, during our break, the student sitting next to me asked what I thought of the book's ending. I felt embarrassed to admit I hadn't read it—everyone else seemed to have read it—so I said, "I hated it."

She asked, "Oh? Why?"

I said, "Because I don't like books about people killing themselves."

Again she asked, "Why?"

Rather than tell her, *Because my little sister just attempted suicide*, I said, "Because I want to live forever, and I want everyone else to live forever too."

She laughed, but I wasn't joking.

I got coffee between classes. I ran into Mo's roommate, Faisal, in the café line. He waved at me. He was standing with a girl I hadn't met before. He introduced me to her as "That girl Mo always talks about."

She grinned. "Oh, you're Margit?"

I forget what Faisal said her name was, because my mind felt like it was full of smoke.

Faisal invited me to hang out with them and Mo later. I said I'd try to stop by but that I might be busy studying.

Every night this week I sat with my schoolbooks open and stared at the words like they were abstract art. I tried to memorize character and author names, but instead I've spent each night listening to arguments happening above me, while I chewed on my fingernails and questioned whether I actually exist.

––––––

"Revolution is about creation, not destruction."

That's what some guy in my American Lit class said today. We're reading *The Grapes of Wrath*. I haven't started it.

I was nodding off in class.

Another guy disagreed. He said, "I actually think we need to burn it all down."

I didn't understand what they were talking about, but I tried to take notes in case I will later.

––––––

The man upstairs was once again on his bullshit last night. Their fights are becoming more frequent. It used to happen once a month, then once every other week. Now it feels like it's every day.

He was yelling at his girlfriend, "*You don't love me!*"

I can't imagine how anyone could resist loving a man who yells at them so often. It sounds like he punches holes in the walls of their rented apartment.

I find it so strange that he is responding to her supposed lack of love for him with violence. It seems so counterintuitive. If I worried someone didn't love me, I would sink into myself. I would become as small as possible. I would be silent. Inoffensive.

Why does he behave like that? What is his goal? Does he think through his actions at all, or does he just act on his angry compulsions?

––––––

Mo called me. I didn't answer. He left a message.

It said, "*Hey Margit, this is Mo. Faisal told me he ran into you. He said you seemed a little off. Exam season is rough, right? Let me know if I can bring you a pizza, or something. I could do a coffee run. You like an Americano with soy milk, right? Give me a call if you have a free minute. No worries if you don't. I totally get that you're busy. Talk to you later.*"

I cried on the bus. People looked at me. I had to lie to the passenger sitting next to me. They asked me if I was okay. I said my dad died.

Of course he didn't really die. I just needed to explain my odd behavior. People don't think you're weird for crying on the bus when your dad dies.

The person who asked me held my hand. I didn't want my hand held, but they didn't know what else to do, so I let them. Sometimes it's kinder to let people believe they are helping you even when they aren't.

My Russian Lit prof picked on me again to answer a question. There was a full room of eager students, all chomping at the bit, and yet he keeps picking me. Every time he points at me, I say, "I don't know, sir."

Does he want to pick someone who doesn't know? Is that the point? Does he like seeing someone squirm? I can't imagine wanting to make someone uncomfortable. I would never ask someone a question I suspected they didn't know the answer to.

Maybe he hasn't prepared enough material to teach, and calling on me eats up time and brings us to the end faster.

I asked, "Are you trying to get to the end faster?"

People shifted in their chairs to look at me.

He tilted his head. "Do you mean the end of the novel?"

I glanced at everyone staring at me. Some of them were muttering.

"Yes," I said, even though that's not what I meant.

There ain't no sin and there ain't no virtue. There's just stuff people do.

That is a significant quote for my American lit class, apparently. I am struggling in that class. I'm struggling in all my classes; however, American Lit is especially painful. Two male students keep monopolizing the conversation. They argue about what agenda they think the author of this book had, while our professor fruitlessly tries to bring the conversation back to the intent of her original lecture. The men say words like "bourgeoisie" a lot.

Today one said, "If you think Steinbeck was a commie, this conversation is pointless."

The other said, "I'm just saying there is a working class and there's a ruling class. The only way to overcome today's problems is to confront the divide between those classes, and it'll have to be violent."

The other man seemed to disagree. He said, "You think that's what this book is saying?"

The other one replied, "I don't care what this book is saying. I care about who I'm supposed to shoot."

People laughed. I didn't understand.

A woman in the class who was paying more attention than I was to their conversation, interjected. She said, "The point is, our actions don't just have to be violent; they should also include positive acts of improving the human condition."

Another student said, "We're way beyond that."

She disagreed. "No we're not. Did you read the same book as me?"

I felt completely lost. I was trying to take notes. I turned to her. "So, wait. Are you saying this book is about violence?"

She said, "Yes, and it's about helping people."

Five

This morning when I left my room, I stepped in sliced mango. Sadiyah must have left it outside my door yesterday, but I didn't notice. I went to my room after school and stayed locked inside until morning.

I washed the mango juice from my foot in the sink. As I scrubbed between my toes, I thought about how sad it is for a tree to grow old enough to bear fruit, to grow that fruit, for that fruit to be picked, for it to be shipped across the world, placed on a shelf by some human in the produce department, purchased, washed, and sliced up by my friend, left to brown outside my door, and then stomped on by me.

I stood balancing with my wet foot in the sink while tears formed in my eyes at the thought of wasted mango. I glanced at myself in the mirror, contorted and crying, and I frowned.

Something is wrong with me. I'm not thinking the way I used to.

I feel foggy-headed, and sad. I think I might be having a hormonal problem. I keep waking up and gasping in the night.

I know that I'm upset about Sigrid, but she's okay—so why am I still like this? I can't get back to normal. I feel out of sorts. She's been awake for over a week now, and I feel worse than I did before. Why?

I took a pregnancy test. I haven't had sex in well over six months, but I catastrophized that maybe I sat on some sperm, or something. That would explain feeling so off, wouldn't it? Pregnant people always feel off, right?

Sometimes having a physical feeling isn't a sign of illness. Sometimes it's just a sign of experiencing something corporeal, like pregnancy. It doesn't mean you have cancer, or anything. It just means that you exist.

I exist, right? I'm alive right now?

I called Sigrid. I said, "We're both alive, right?"

She replied, "Jesus Christ, I'm about to tell the hospital to block your calls. I'm in a facility that doesn't have doors on the bathrooms. Do you realize that? I'm not allowed floss or to use silverware. They give us these flimsy wooden sporks. Please, stop calling me and talking to me like you're the one who is nuts. Bring me my goddamn phone. Please. I can't find it anywhere. I'm alive, okay? I am not dead. I'm alive. I'm alive. I'm alive—"

"Are you going to die?" I asked.

I was sitting on the floor of my closet. I didn't want my roommates to overhear.

She exhaled. "I mean, yeah? We all die, right?"

"Are you going to try to kill yourself again?"

Last night, I read that having one suicide attempt is the highest indicator that someone will die by suicide.

She paused, then said, "No."

"How do I know you're not lying?"

She said, "You just have to trust me, I guess."

"You want me to trust you?" I asked.

She said, "I don't want you to do anything besides bring me my phone."

Jerry and my parents are mad at me because I didn't tell them Sigrid was hospitalized. I found her. I called 911. I was listed as her next of kin. I stayed with her until she woke up.

When she woke up, I called my mom. I told her Sigrid was okay, but she was in the hospital. She tried to ask me questions, but I said I didn't feel well, and could we talk later. I hadn't slept in days. I wanted to go home. I'd missed a lot of school. I gave her the room number, then I left. I drove home crying. I saw a truck upside down in the ditch.

I wonder if the driver was okay. I hope they didn't die.

I have been ignoring Jerry's calls. I picked up once, but she was irate. She asked me why I didn't tell them about Sigrid earlier. She told me they had spoken to her nurses and found out I'd been there all week. She said they were furious that I kept this from them. *"Who do you think you are? What gives you the right?"*

I told her I wanted to spare everyone the horror of the in-between. I resisted the urge to yell back at her. I felt angry; I wanted to say, *Fuck you, Jerry. Why do you think she tried to kill herself? You aren't blameless.* I bit my tongue instead. I restrained myself.

She said, *"The horror of the in-between? What the hell does that mean?"*

I explained that I didn't want to upset her or my parents

unnecessarily before I knew they had to be upset. I said that when someone is hurt, or dies, you are supposed to wait as long as possible to inform others, to preserve every moment they could have without the heartache. Once you find out something terrible, there's no erasing it. Terrible things stick to you forever.

"I wanted to spare you," I said.

That wasn't the whole truth. I was putting it off. I didn't know what to say. I didn't have the note ready. I also partly blamed them, and I couldn't stomach the idea of speaking to any of them. I worried I might say something I'd regret.

"You didn't have the right to do that," Jerry said. *"You aren't God, Margit."*

I wanted to say, *I know I'm not God, Jerry. If I were God, things would be different,* but instead I said, *"I know. I'm sorry."*

Six

I feel like I have food poisoning, but I haven't eaten anything. My stomach is churning, and I have a fever.

I had food poisoning once before. I ate questionable chicken. I recall retching into a toilet, beseeching God to spare me from further agony. I begged him out loud. My voice echoed in the porcelain bowl. I pleaded that if he cured me, I would do anything. I would dedicate my life to him. I would become a nun. If he stopped my suffering, I would spend the rest of my days on my knees at a pew, wearing a habit, kissing crucifixes, praising his holy name.

I am not a nun. I am an English major, and not a very good one. I didn't follow through on my promise. In fact, lately I've been questioning whether God exists at all. I feel suspended between suspecting God is bogus and worrying that I'm being punished for thinking that, and for lying to him.

Maybe that's why I feel sick. Maybe that's why everything feels
so terrible right now.

God, if you exist and you're mad at me, I'm sorry. I wouldn't
have made a good nun. Every nun I've ever met has been resolute
and unemotional. I am the opposite of that. Furthermore, a defining
characteristic of nunship is a profound understanding of sisterhood,
and I feel profoundly oblivious when it comes to that.

Today the angry man who lives above me was muttering into his
phone on his balcony. I was beneath him on mine. I thought fresh
air might make me feel better. He was hushing to a woman, who was
clearly not his girlfriend, that he loved her legs.

Sadiyah was sitting outside with me. She was aghast. She kept
whispering, "*Oh my God. He's totally cheating on his girlfriend.*"

I felt like an abused chicken on the bottom of stacked cages at a
chicken farm, who was being shit on by all the chickens above her.
I felt repulsed by his voice, and for being exposed to what I was beginning to worry was a leg fetish. I tried to tune him out so I could
study, but he was going on and on about the curve of this woman's
calves and ankles.

Sadiyah had both her hands cupping her cheeks. She kept
mouthing, *Oh my God.*

I just wanted to study in peace. I couldn't focus with him above
us. I felt sick. So I got up and went to my bedroom. I shut my door
and paused.

I wanted to throw up. I could hear the woman above me crying.

I almost barfed on the floor. I crouched down. I felt my stomach
churn and cold sweat develop on my forehead. I considered begging
God to spare me. I lay down on my back, looked up at the dusty
light fixture in my ceiling, and tried to think of a bargain I could
make with God.

Before Sigrid was in the hospital, I spent a lot of time thinking about Mo. I woke up with him on my mind before I even opened my eyes. I'd look at my phone every morning, hoping he'd texted me. He always had. He works part-time as a security guard at the mall to pay for school, and I used to go pretend I needed to shop, but really, I just wanted to run into him.

My mind hasn't been on Mo since Sigrid's attempt. I've barely thought of him. Now that I'm beginning to again, I realize how bizarre it is for me to waste so much of my time worrying about how much he likes me. It's strange to think of myself feeling nervous that he'll stop texting me. I overanalyzed his messages and talked to my friends ad nauseam about whether he would ever finally ask me out.

I am on the floor of the bathroom hurling into the toilet.

There are trucks upside down in ditches.

People are dying in hospitals.

I called Mo and asked him to be my boyfriend. I was on the bathroom floor, straddling the toilet. I kept retching and spitting into the bowl, but I had nothing in my stomach to throw up. I had my phone up to my ear, and a line of spit strung from my mouth into the toilet.

I told God I'd ask Mo to be my boyfriend if he'd make me feel better. I figured that God was probably sick of me bugging him about Mo in my prayers.

Mo laughed. "What? I thought you weren't interested."

I brushed my hair out of my sweaty face and said, "No, I like you a lot."

He asked what compelled me to ask him to be my boyfriend, and I said, "Just because." However, the truth is I wanted to feel

something good. I felt so profoundly ill that I thought maybe if
Mo said he wanted to be my boyfriend, I might feel a little better.

He said, "I'd kill to be your boyfriend. I'm surprised you're asking
me, though. You've been kind of distant lately. I was worried about
you. Is school really weighing on you right now, or something?
What's been going on?"

I said, "Yes, and there's some other things."

"Like what?" he asked.

Rather than tell him about Sigrid, I told him I was very sick, I
stepped in mango, and it made me cry. I also told him about the couple above me. I said the guy is cheating and they're always fighting. It
was keeping me up at night. I said, "I'm worried about the woman.
The guy sounds really aggressive."

He suggested maybe I should call someone.

I said, "Is that what I'm supposed to do?"

He said, "I don't know."

My mom left me a voicemail message. In an angry voice she asked,
"*Do you have your sister's phone?*" I didn't feel like talking to her after
everything that happened with Sigrid. Rather than return her call,
I texted her. I wanted to write, *Don't leave me angry messages*, but
instead I wrote,

I don't have sig's phone. sorry.

She replied,

How are we supposed to trust you? Are you lying?

Rather than write back, Fuck off, I wrote,

I'm not lying, mom.

After my grandma died, I found myself scowling at old women. I felt affronted by their existence. I know that's unreasonable. It's ridiculous. But when I saw any lady over eighty, I thought, *Fuck you. Why are you alive when my grandma isn't? Do you deserve to be here more than her?*

I went to Walmart to buy nylons for her funeral. Before I got out of the car, I watched an old lady hobble through the parking lot as if she murdered my grandma with her own arthritic hands. I gripped the steering wheel and felt incensed at the sight of this frail, elderly woman. I had to take deep breaths.

After the initial blow of her death, I got over hating old women. I convinced myself I was being ridiculous. I decided it was just a weird reaction to my grief.

I had never felt anything like that before. It was strange for my worldview to shift like that. I didn't realize I could think so differently, and in a way that left me feeling disturbed.

I wonder if old people are often crotchety because they've dealt with so many atrocities, they can no longer tolerate anyone. Maybe they ask to speak to managers, hold up lines, and drive at a snail's pace because they're at the end of their ropes. Maybe all their people have died, gotten sick, or tried to kill themselves, and it's irksome to see the rest of us tottering around, breathing air, taking up space.

I called Mo again and told him my theory about old people. I told him I hope I don't feel like that when I'm old. I don't want to scowl at children. I don't want to feel resentful of other people for just existing. I want to do the opposite. I want to appreciate people.

I didn't tell Mo this, but last week, when Sigrid was in the hospital, I worried I was going to feel that way again. I worried I'd walk around hating people who reminded me of her. That would include: any young woman, people who smoke, lesbians, imaginative people, anyone with a tattoo, people with ADD, opinionated people, anyone with no social filter, little girls holding toys, anyone laughing, and people with sisters.

Mo said, "Some old people are nice."

He then told me about his great-aunt. Her name is Aida. "Nicest lady you'll ever meet," he said. "Always chatting with strangers. Gives everyone a dollar. And she's always finding injured baby animals and helping them. She feeds them with this water dropper. She's like ninety years old, and she's always nursing baby rabbits and birds."

Drysdale is live streaming the mayoral debate. The election is next week. I am lying next to Mo in my bed, and we're watching the candidates discuss whether libraries should have gay picture books in them.

Mo has never been to Drysdale, but I've told him about it. Once, at a party, while I was crying to him about my childhood, he said he'd like to visit Drysdale with me. He said he wants to see where I grew up. He asked if we could go for a drive sometime. He told me he was interested in small towns. He's a geography student.

Regarding the gay picture books, Kevin said, "*They should be removed.*"

Another candidate named Desmond said, "*They should be put someplace separate from the other books. On a shelf you have to request access for.*"

A candidate name Lisa, who has absolutely no chance of winning, said, "*Yes, of course, we need those on the shelves.*"

Mo said, "Well, I hope Lisa wins."

I assured him, "She won't."

Seven

Mo and I fell asleep watching the debate. We woke up at two a.m. to the couple above us fighting. It sounded like the man just got home. His girlfriend was confronting him. She cried, "*Where were you?*"

He yelled, "*I was working! Leave me alone! It's none of your business!*"

I turned on my bedside light, and Mo and I looked at each other with concern. After about five minutes of listening to their shouting escalate, Mo climbed out of bed. He started putting his socks on.

He said, "I think I have to go up there."

Just as he reached for the doorknob, we could hear them calming down.

The man said, "*I'm sorry.*"

Sigrid was released from inpatient care yesterday. Jerry and my parents pooled some money to pay for an outpatient psychiatrist. It's expensive, I guess. She's going to move out of her apartment and stay at Mom and Dad's for a while. I drove to Drysdale to help her pack, despite needing to study for an exam tomorrow.

I hadn't seen her since the hospital. I thought maybe I might hug her or say something important, but I didn't. I looked at her, she looked at me, and we nodded.

She asked me if I had her phone. I said, "No. Sorry. I don't."

While we assembled boxes and packed up her things, she asked, "Did you clean up in here while I was in the hospital?"

I said, "I don't remember."

She frowned.

I noticed the bag she brought with her had a journal in it.

I asked, "Are you keeping a diary?"

She said, "Yeah, they asked me to in therapy. I can't find my old journal. Did you take it?"

I said no, even though I did, and asked what else they told her to do.

She said they taught her coping mechanisms. They have her do some exercises with her eyes. When she told me that, I worried she was working with a quack, so I googled it. Apparently, it's a medically sound and evidenced-based form of therapy. I guess certain eye movements facilitate brain healing. It might mimic what our eyes do during REM sleep.

Sigrid and I are both sleeping in our old bedroom tonight. I decided to stay over, rather than drive the forty minutes home. I said I felt too tired to drive, but the truth is I didn't feel tired. I just wanted to stay.

My parents confronted me earlier. They said, "We're very disappointed in how you handled this."

I said, "I'm disappointed too," but secretly I didn't mean that

I was disappointed in myself. I felt disappointed by the whole circumstance—by them, by Sigrid, by God.

Our room doesn't have bunk beds anymore, so I slept on a mattress on the floor. Sigrid was beside me, in a twin-sized bed. Other than that, the room is the same as it was when we were kids. The same curtains are draped over the windows. The same pink paint is on the walls. My prom dress hangs in the closet. There are bumps in the plaster where Dad punched a hole in our wall.

I couldn't sleep. I lay awake in the darkness, listening to Sigrid inhale and exhale.

The streetlights cast a glow through the lace pattern in the curtains. There's this shadow that sways on the wall, which I completely forgot about until last night. I used to fall asleep watching it sway back and forth.

My dad opened our door at one a.m. He opened it quietly, without realizing I was awake. He stood in the doorframe and looked at us before shutting it.

My mom did the same thing at three a.m.

Sigrid snored, and I thought maybe I should go get my parents. Maybe they'd like to hear her.

I realized that was weird and stopped myself.

I felt out of it. I still do. I wish I could snap out of this feeling.

I kept opening and closing my eyes.

I wondered what eye movements facilitate brain healing.

I kept blinking. Widening them as far as I could.

I prayed in the hospital that Sigrid would wake up. I clenched every muscle in my body. I strained my face and neck while I willed, with every ounce of myself, that she'd wake up. I felt like I might crack a molar from gritting my teeth so tightly, praying, *Wake up. Wake up.*

I didn't think she would wake up the last day. I thought for sure she'd die. I thought there was no way this was going to end well. I'm still not sure if it will.

I got up at five a.m. to drive back to school. Sigrid was still snoring. Before leaving, I put the note I wrote for her on her chest.

My parents were awake. My mom was making coffee. My dad was tinkering with a radio on the kitchen table. I considered telling them I was angry at them, but I didn't.

I said, "Bye, guys. See you later."

They said, "Bye, Margit. Drive safely."

Eight

My Russian lit professor approached me after I submitted my exam.

He followed me into the hall and said, "Margit? Can I have a word with you please?"

I thought he was going to confront me about how badly I've let my grades slip, or how he could tell I failed the midterm just by glancing at it, but he didn't.

He said, "Is everything okay?"

I nodded instinctively. I said, "Yes, why?"

He said, "I've noticed a change with you in class in the last few weeks. I've been concerned. I wanted to reach out."

"Oh," I said.

Is that why he kept calling on me? He noticed something was wrong with me? I didn't realize my professors paid attention to my disengagement in class. When I watch a prof give a lecture, it feels like watching a performance. When I'm in an audience, I've never considered that the performer might be watching me too.

"I've been having some personal troubles," I confessed.

He nodded. "Yes, I thought so. How did you find the midterm?"

I shrugged. I had tears in my eyes.

He said, "I think we should arrange an alternate test for you, for later. What do you think? We have support resources at the school. You've probably heard your other professors peddling them, but they're good. Really. I want to give you some phone numbers, okay?"

I called the number he gave me from a school bathroom. I spoke to a counselor. I told her my professor suggested I call, and then rambled about what's been going on. She listened to me, then said, "I'm so sorry you're going through this." She took my information and said she would arrange for a school psychologist. She also suggested I go to a walk-in, get a doctor's note, and defer the rest of my midterms.

Before hanging up, she asked, "Do you have a support system?"

I said, "Yes. I have roommates, and friends, and a boyfriend."

She said, "Having a community is important. Have you talked about what you're going through with them?"

I said, "Not really, no. Not about my sister."

She suggested I consider telling them.

I was in the waiting room at the walk-in when Sigrid called me.

She said, "Hey. I read the note."

I didn't want to talk much, to avoid bothering the patients sitting around me, so I said, "Okay."

She said, "I'm sorry for asking you to write that."

I said, "It's okay."

"I'm sorry, period," she said.

"It's okay."

"I won't do it again."

"Okay."

"I really won't."

"Okay."

I sat on the examination table and read the posters on the wall. One showed the anatomy of the female reproductive system. Another promoted the HPV vaccine. There was also a printed piece of paper pinned to the wall. It said: DOCTOR'S NOTES ARE $50.00.

When the doctor came into the examination room, I felt nervous. I felt like a fraud, trying to get out of doing my homework. Despite being directed here by school employees, I still felt guilty somehow.

She asked what brought me in, and I stammered.

I said, "I-I'm having mental health problems."

I thought she'd look at me like I was a con artist. It's exam season; it's the time of year when students come to doctors for notes.

She didn't look at me like that, though. She said, "Oh, I'm so sorry to hear that," with sincerity in her voice.

I involuntarily cried in response. I felt like I just drank two bottles of wine; I lost my filter and felt myself unloading all my sorrows on her—the way I have with my friends in the cabs or bar bathrooms. I felt beside myself. I told her my professor noticed something was wrong with me, and a school counselor suggested I get a note. I blurted out that my sister tried to kill herself, and that I was struggling to do anything. I said I couldn't study. I couldn't sleep.

She listened to me intently, handed me tissues, and then wrote me a note. She told me it's best not to worry about school right now. Focus on myself. She gave me a prescription sleeping pill and said, "I'm really sorry you're going through this."

"That's okay," I said, which was weird of me. I should have said, "Thank you," or something. I wasn't expecting her to be so nice or understanding. I went there thinking I'd have to argue with the doctor. I came prepared to convince her I was telling the truth. I tend to expect conflict. I brace myself for hostility, so I feel flustered and unprepared when people are kind to me.

Before leaving her office, I stopped at the receptionist's desk to pay for the note. The receptionist waved me off. He said, "The doctor said no charge."

I called Mo from my car. I was beside myself. I blubbered to him about Sigrid and deferring my exams. I cried that I was sorry for not telling him sooner, but that's why I've been so weird.

He came over to my apartment right away. He was waiting at the door before I arrived home. I noticed his shirt was on backward. I think he threw it on without looking as he hurried over.

We sat in the living room, where I continued to sob to him about what's been going on. I told him I feel outside my body. I said I felt sick, like the world is fake and I need help.

Candace and Sadiyah were at the library studying, but they came home unexpectedly. I think Mo texted them.

They sat with us, and I repeated what I'd told Mo.

Sadiyah said, "We thought something was wrong."

Candace nodded. "We've been worried. We didn't know what to do. I'm sorry."

Nine

Mo and I went for a drive and ended up in Drysdale. We drove up and down Main Street. I pointed out my old high school and the laundromat I worked at. We drove by my grandma's old house, and the old movie theater. I said, "That's where I had my first date."

I told him my stories about being a kid in Drysdale. He slowed down whenever I had something to say. He listened to me, rapt, while I pointed out a play structure where I broke my arm. He looked with interest at the house where I played spin the bottle, and laughed when I told him I'd punched a boy in the face there for calling my friend June a slut.

We drove by the hospital, and I didn't say anything about it, but he put his hand on my leg and squeezed while we drove past.

We pulled over outside my parents' place. It was nighttime and all the lights were off. We got out of the car, leaned on the hood, and stared at the house. It looked smaller than usual.

I pointed out the windows in the basement. I told him, "A raccoon broke in once."

We stared until a car pulled up. I couldn't tell who was driving because it had its brights on, but by the time it parked, I saw it was Sigrid.

She climbed out of the car with a cigarette in her mouth. She approached us and said, "Is that Marg? What are you doing here?"

She looked at Mo and said, "Who are you?"

I caught myself before correcting her. I almost said, *That's not a polite way to ask someone their name.*

Instead, I let Mo introduce himself. He shook her hand. "Nice to meet you. I'm Mo."

"Who's Mo?" she asked me, while still shaking his hand.

Again I resisted the urge to correct her. I said, "He's my boyfriend."

I told Mo, "This is my sister."

She looked at him and said, "Boyfriend. No way. How long has this been going on?"

"Not very long," he said. "A week officially, but we've known each other all year."

"Did she tell you about me?" she asked.

It was dark, but I could tell Mo felt awkward. He probably wasn't sure what she meant. *Did I tell him about her in general, or about her recent suicide attempt?*

I wanted to jump in to guide his answer. I wanted to cue him into the safer assumption being that I told him about her in general, but before I could, Mo said, "Yeah, she told me she loves you."

Sigrid laughed.

Ten

I went to my first therapy session today. It was exhausting. I mostly just unloaded on the doctor. She took notes and assured me she can help me.

She told me people who grow up in houses with volatile parents can become hypervigilant toward fluctuations in other people's moods to protect themselves. I told her how I used to nudge Sigrid's ribs when I noticed tension rising.

She said, "It sounds like you were trying to protect your sister, too."

We talked about how I used to do Sigrid's homework. She acknowledged that I was a kid with good intentions; however, that wasn't the best way to help her.

I asked, "Then what *is* the best way to help her?"

She said, "I'm not sure. Have you asked her?"

We have another session booked later this week.

When I got home, I tried to take a nap, but I couldn't. I heard screaming and a door slam above me. The man was yelling, "*Come back here!*" It sounded worse than usual. It sounded like his girlfriend was trying to get away. She was shrieking, "*No! Leave me alone! You're hurting me!*"

I didn't know what to do. I texted Mo.

It sounds bad upstairs. What should i do?

He was in an exam. He didn't read my text.

It sounds like someone is fighting above us, I texted the group chat with my roommates.

They were studying. They weren't looking at their phones.

I stood in my room with my hand on my chest. The woman screamed again. I hesitated, then darted out of my room and out of the apartment. I rushed up the stairs.

Their door was open. The girl was in the doorframe, trying to leave. The guy was yanking her arm, not letting her go.

"Leave her alone!" I shouted down the hall.

She looked up at me, and he let go of her.

"This isn't what it looks like," he said.

"Just leave her alone," I repeated.

He let go and slammed the door shut.

She straightened herself, walked toward me, and we both reached out our hands.

I invited her to follow me to my apartment. She nodded and came with me down the stairs. I brought her right into my bedroom because that felt safer somehow. I could lock the apartment door, and my bedroom door.

He had torn her shirt, and she was crying. She looked disheveled and distressed.

I left her in my room for a moment to get her a glass of water.

When I returned, I handed it to her and I asked if she was okay.

She said, "I'm okay. Thank you. It's weird. I can hear him pacing over your room, I think. I can hear him talking on his phone."

I nodded. "Yes, the floors are thin. I've been hearing you for a while. I was really worried about you."

"I should have known that," she said. "I can hear you too."

"What do you mean?" I frowned.

"I heard you crying the last couple weeks. I was concerned about you, too. Are you okay?"

The girl's name is Isabelle. She and I lay on my bedroom floor, listening to the floorboards creak above us. She told me she and Dan had broken up a number of times already, but this was the last time.

"It's really the last time," she said, as if I wouldn't believe her.

She asked me if I had been crying about a boy, and I said no.

I told her about Sigrid. I told her how she'd tried to kill herself, and how I sat with her in the hospital for five days. I told her about how Jerry and my parents were mad at me, and how I'm struggling in all my classes and have had to defer my exams. I told her Mo and my friends were worried, and that I just started therapy.

She said, "It sounds like a lot of people want to help you."

I nodded. I am lucky to have people who notice when I'm not doing well, and who want to help me. Not everyone has that.

I asked, "Do you have people who want to help you?"

She said, "I don't think anyone knows I need help."

I didn't know Sigrid needed help. There was this distance between us. When I first moved out, I felt like I'd abandoned her. I left her alone in that house with our parents. I found it difficult to talk to her. I felt guilty.

But I was eager to move out. I wanted to get away. I loved living in the dorms my first year. I loved moving into my apartment with Candace and Sadiyah. I felt free. I grew up walking on eggshells. I felt constantly drained and overwhelmed. It was a relief to live somewhere new, to take classes I liked, to have my own room, and to live with people who were calm and easy to be around.

Sigrid and I never got along. We were never friends. We lived in the same space, endured the same parental trauma, ate the same Ritz-cracker-encrusted food, and felt the same grief when our grandma died. We were sisters.

I cried for a week after I was dumped by a guy who looked like a blobfish. Sigrid had to sleep in our bedroom with me while I sobbed into my pillow. She and I were in a fight. The fight was trivial, but I was mad. I was giving her the silent treatment.

After seven days of crying, I woke up to a text from my ex that said,

Did you egg my house?

I laughed. I knew immediately that Sigrid had done it. While I kept her up with my crying and ignored her, she tracked down his address, purchased or stole eggs, walked down his street with a carton, and flung them at his house.

After reading his text, I looked down at her. She was asleep in the bunk bed beneath me. Her mouth ajar. She was exhausted from her evening out egging boys who were mean to me.

Even when she and I were fighting, or hadn't spoken in months, there has never been a time when I would hesitate to bury a body for her.

I was so disappointed in her for not graduating high school. She used to talk my ear off in our bedroom about moving away, getting out of Drysdale and living some weird, exciting life. I knew she was capable of doing that. It bothered me that she had no follow-through. I wondered if I could have done something, controlled her in some way, to force her to make better choices.

I couldn't talk to her. I felt this mixture of guilt, disappointment, resentment, and care for her. I don't know how to communicate with someone when I have negative or complicated feelings for them. She and I always fought. To my credit, the communication skills modeled for us involved screaming and punching drywall. I didn't know what to say.

I had no idea what was going on in her life. I didn't know she felt so isolated. I didn't know about Greta's drug problem. I didn't know how troubled or alone she felt. I didn't realize she was depressed. I didn't realize how sensitive she felt about our family. I wish I'd known. I wish I'd asked.

I asked Isabelle, "What can I do to help you?"

She and I stayed in my room for hours. She wanted to hear Dan leave, so we could go back upstairs and collect her belongings. She made plans to stay at her mom's house. She didn't want to risk going up while he was still there. She wanted to be sure he was out of the house. She didn't want to abandon all her things. All her photos were in the apartment. All her clothes.

"Maybe we can smoke him out," she said.

I nodded. "I have an idea," and texted Mo.

Mo knocked on the door wearing his security guard uniform.

Dan peeked his head out into the hall and said, "Can I help you?"

Mo said, "We need to evacuate the building. There's been a bomb threat."

My roommates and neighbors were in on it. I texted them about what was happening. We all stood outside across the street. Isabelle was inside hiding.

Dan frowned. "A bomb threat? What?"

Mo said, "Yes, we all need to get out of the building immediately."

Dan said, "Is this a prank threat? Who the hell would bomb a fourplex? What the fuck—"

Mo said, "Making bomb threats is a criminal offense. It doesn't matter if it's real or a hoax. Don't touch anything. Don't stand near the windows. We have to get out of here as calmly as possible."

He followed Mo outside.

Sigrid

One

Dr. Jeong said writing will help me process my thoughts and feelings. I warned her I'm a bad writer, that I failed high school English, but she said that didn't matter. Do it anyway.

Apparently, writing helps us work through our painful experiences. According to her, research suggests that writing about our life's traumatic moments can help us learn and develop coping skills.

I'm not sure I buy that, but I'm not a doctor. I don't know if she's going to read this, or if I'm just writing it for myself. It feels like homework. Actually, it feels lousier than homework. I'd rather write about Magellan than about my own traumatic memories. This exercise involves dwelling on topics that make me feel bad, and it exposes my shoddy writing abilities, which are embarrassing. I'm not sure why a psychologist would recommend torturing a person who recently attempted suicide, but I'm uneducated. Lowbrow.

Anti-intellectual. A philistine, I think. I'm not confident I know what the word "philistine" means, but you get me, right? I'm boneheaded.

Maybe I should erase that. I bet therapists don't take kindly to their patients being self-deprecating. God only knows what torture I'd be in for if Dr. Jeong gets wind that I'm deeply insecure.

I told her I'd rather write about the moon, but she gave me a look my teachers used to give me, which means, *Just do what I say.*

I think the moon is a woman. People always say, "the man in the moon," but there's no way the moon is a dude. She's got a soulful face. She's gorgeous. In French, the moon is a feminine word. The sun is a man, but the moon—la lune—she's a lady.

It was courteous of me to say I'd rather write about the moon than write this, because the truth is I'd rather write about garbage. I'd rather write about human shit. I was polite enough to not say that to Dr. J. because, like the moon, I am also a lady.

Part of why I feel rotten about this therapy assignment is because I've actually written about all this before. I kept a detailed diary. I don't think that ever helped me. In fact, it may have contributed to my issues. I got way too in my head. Depressed. Maybe I was doing it wrong. I'm not sure. I'm not confident that I know how to do anything properly. I'm trying to keep this a secret from my doctor, but the truth is I am profoundly self-conscious and pretty convinced that I'm dumb.

I wish I could show Dr. Jeong my old journal so she could tell me where I went wrong, but I think my sister stole it. I can't find it anywhere.   •

We don't actually get much choice in life, do we? I used to think I could do anything, but that's not really how things work. It's a facade. The truth is we get very little wiggle room. We're born where we are, with the bodies we have, the smarts we've got, and our destinies all mapped out. It's preordained, or at least I think it is.

I have to do what I'm asked to do. There is no escape.

In the twelfth grade, my friend Greta went to a party without me. I said I had the flu, but I lied. I just wasn't up for it. I felt lazy. She went alone, drank a lot, and started feeling sick. She puked in the backyard, then wandered through the house until she found an empty bedroom to sleep in.

I know this because she told me the following Monday. She said she woke up hours later to a boy asleep beside her. She assumed it was his room. She watched his chest move up and down in the dark. She thought he looked peaceful. She felt warmth radiate from him and listened to him breathe. In the same way that puppy litters cuddle, she curled into him and nodded back to sleep.

She and I used to do that when I slept over at her place. It was platonic; it felt like we were drowsy baby creatures in a nest. Little pink baby rats, or ugly little birds.

She woke up later to his head shoved between her jaw and collar bone. He was on top of her. Startled, she said, "I'm gay." She was shocked, both by what was happening, and by what came out of her mouth. She had never said that she was gay out loud before—not even to me.

That was her way of saying no, but I guess it wasn't clear enough. I guess the guy thought she was just irrelevantly coming out to him.

In the morning, everyone who slept over walked to get breakfast at the diner around the corner. He sat across from her. She ordered blueberry pancakes, and they discussed movies. They joked.

As far as I know, she's never told anyone this story except me. At first, she didn't give me all the details. She just said she woke up and he was on top of her. She said that casually. Her tone was light. It was as if she were talking about something less serious. She said nonchalantly, *"Well, a gross thing happened to me at the party."*

I remember looking at her after she said that. I said, *"That's really gross. Maybe we should go to the hospital."*

It'd been two days. She said she had already showered forty times. *"We could still go,"* I said.

She said no, she didn't want to.

I felt so guilty about not going to that party. I still think about it. When people ask me, *"What's your biggest regret?"* I say, *"I didn't go to a party once,"* and they think I'm being funny.

She had her dad's car that day at school. At lunch she drove us to McDonald's. On the way there, I asked her to stop at a pharmacy. I got myself a scratch card and bought her the morning after pill. I tossed it at her and said, *"You might as well take that."* Then quickly changed the subject. I said, *"Should we get chocolate or strawberry milkshakes?"*

She said, *"Chocolate,"* while she swallowed the pill dry.

We ate in the school parking lot. While we downed our milkshakes and split a large fry, she announced, *"I think I'm gay."*

I choked on my food.

She explained that she had said that to the guy at the party instead of no. She told me she had been thinking it for a while, but was pretty sure now.

I said, *"You're gay? Really?"*

She nodded. She seemed worried about how I'd react.

I started laughing. I almost choked on a fry.

She said, *"What?"*

"You won't believe it," I said.

"What?" she asked again.

Then I told her, *"I am too."*

It was obvious we were gay in retrospect. She and I used to pick boys to have crushes on. I thought of it like a game. She picked a guy named Ethan because he knew how to play guitar. I picked a guy named Josh because he was good at math. I thought that was impressive. At one point, we switched crushes because Ethan became a vegetarian and Greta couldn't give up pepperoni.

For a while, she and I only liked listening to music sung by men. I worried we did that because of internalized misogyny, or something, but Greta pointed out that we probably just preferred hearing songs about loving women. Neither of us enjoyed songs about being into men.

There is this magnetism between queer kids. It's a weird phenomenon; we find each other even before we realize we're queer. Greta and I were never attracted to each other; it wasn't that we sensed some romantic tension, or anything like that. We just gravitated toward each other as friends because, on some invisible level, there was a special link between us. Though I like to believe we would have been friends even if we weren't lesbians.

Greta taught me a lot of things. After she and I realized we were gay, she got really into reading about it. She became a fan of lesbian poets and started reading queer theory. She read a lot about racism, politics, feminism, and history. Sometimes, she would come to school and read me facts she'd learned. I remember her telling me the world's oldest porn, which dated back over three thousand years, featured both male-on-male and female-on-female couples.

There used to be a gay brothel on the site where Buckingham Palace is today.

There was a story published twenty-five years before *Dracula* about a Black lesbian vampire who preyed on young women.

After we came out to each other, we told everyone at school. It felt like we had discovered dinosaur bones or solved some complex riddle. We felt obliged to broadcast it. Because we were both in the same predicament, it was easier to announce. We did it together. We said, *"Guess which one of us is gay?"* and then after people tried to guess, we would cackle, *"It's both of us! Can you believe it?"*

After we told everyone, people started to assume we were dating. I remember kids referring to us as girlfriends. We rarely corrected them because it didn't matter. Sometimes, when it happened, we would reply, *"Yeah, sure, we love each other,"* because we did love each other.

Two

Sorry I stopped writing earlier. Thinking about Greta sort of knocks the wind out of me. Is that the point of this? Am I supposed to wrestle with my sadness in this letter? Will that cure me? I don't see that happening. I think I'll be sad about Greta forever. I feel like I'm the only bird left on the planet. I feel like my one bird friend got shot down from the sky. I've been left to live among the monkeys, who don't understand what it's like to grow feathers or lay eggs.

One of the unexpected side effects to being openly gay in a small, conservative, predominantly white community like Drysdale is being a forced spokesperson. You involuntarily become a voice for the queer community. You get this spotlight cast on you that you don't deserve, and that you aren't primed for. You're considered representative. You could be incredibly ignorant, like me, and still—people will start turning to you when certain topics come up. It doesn't just happen for topics relating to conversion therapy and whether gay people should be allowed in the military, either. Eyes were on us when people talked about things like racism, climate change, and abortion, for some faulty reason.

I didn't expect that. I had no idea that would happen. I anticipated facing some homophobic hostility, but you would have to be in the know to prepare yourself to be treated like a constant debate opponent.

Greta and I commiserated about how eyes started turning toward us during certain conversations. Once, we were in a group of people discussing an expensive ramp to be installed at city hall. People were complaining about the cost. They kept glancing at us to see if we would argue with them about it.

Greta did argue. She said sarcastically, *"Oh yeah, fuck ramps. Who wants disabled people in city hall, anyway? Get fucked if you need a ramp, am I right?"*

They called her a "snowflake," and I told them to go fuck themselves.

We didn't handle that situation well, per se, but if I didn't have Greta, I think I would have handled it worse. Maybe I wouldn't have said anything. Maybe I would have nodded along or agreed with them.

Once one of our friends told me, *"You don't look like a lesbian."*

I replied, *"Thank you."*

Greta huffed. She was sitting behind me.

Later, she confronted me. She said, *"You think it's a compliment to not look like a lesbian?"*

I said, *"No, I know it was backhanded, but what did you want me to do? Tell her to fuck off when she's pretending to be nice?"*

"Yes," she said.

Greta pointed out that we were on a podium in a cesspool. She said we had been assigned a task. We were severely underqualified candidates for a campaign she knew was right. Eyes were on us whether they should have been or not. We were morally obligated to be less stupid. We were often asked questions about topics we knew nothing about. People were always fishing for us to condone their shitty beliefs.

I was annoyed by that. It was a burden. I thought it was unfair that on top of dealing with all the horrors of my existence, I had to shoulder responsibilities that were unjustly assigned to me. Other people in Drysdale floundered around in their ignorance, but if I continued to behave like them—like I always had—I would be worse than them because of the podium I was forced on.

By the end of grade twelve, when I slept over at Greta's, I would smoke weed out her window while she lay on her bed and recapped all the things she'd read. For example, she taught me that queer white women are extremely dangerous to more marginalized groups because we're tokenized by white communities and weaponized to make things worse. That's why, for example, transphobic people are often citing white lesbians. Lesbians who condone transphobic beliefs are given this special limelight because they're pawns.

I was a bad student. If left to my own devices, I would have been even more ignorant than I already am. If I hadn't met Greta, I think I would be a totally different person.

A lot of people at school started to find Greta insufferable. She started arguing with people. She once got into a heated debate with our history teacher. He made some offhand ignorant comment about a male student being girly, and she told him that was unacceptable. She stood up from her chair.

Sometimes, she was combative. A lot of people at school started to dislike her. It might surprise some folks to know that she felt the same way about herself. She once said, *"I know I'm unbearable, but what else can I be? We have to be unbearable, you and I."*

I used to joke, *"I wish we were rats"* because, if I could choose how the world worked, we would all be rats at a fair. We would all live well, sampling every possible ounce of happiness. We would roll around in garbage and suck on sour keys.

Three

Jerry hosted Thanksgiving a few months back. At that time, I was sort of spiraling. My grandma had died about two years prior. I barely spoke to anyone in my family. Margit felt like a stranger. Greta and I weren't speaking. I began accepting she was lost. I started carrying Narcan with me everywhere, in case I ran into her. I always pictured her overdosing.

I spent the majority of my free time rereading my past text conversations and email chains with Greta. I liked reading our old banter and remembering how she used to be. She would send me links to interesting articles she'd read.

I read an email she wrote me one October. In it, she shared a link titled, THE TRUE HISTORY OF THANKSGIVING. I didn't read the article when she first sent it. She sent me so many articles, and I was lazy. I didn't like reading like she did. When I revisited our conversation, I read the article. I learned that Thanksgiving is a day of mourning for a lot of Indigenous people. It's a reminder of genocide, and of the continued assault on their people and culture. After reading, I decided I didn't want to celebrate that anymore.

I wasn't sure how to decline when Jerry called to invite me. I considered being honest. The old Greta would have told me to talk to Jerry about this. She said we had to talk to our families about these sorts of things; however, Marg would have nudged me. She would have said I should avoid ruffling feathers.

I knew this would ruffle Jerry's feathers. She would scoff. She would say I was overly sensitive or that I had been brainwashed by the media, or by phony politicians, or by crooked scientists somehow. She would say my political correctness was toxic; I was selfish, and virtue signaling. I would end up getting heated and shouting that I would rather signal virtue than signal hate, or whatever the fuck it was she signaled. The prospect of instigating that argument felt like willingly hopping into the chasm beneath a porta potty.

So I faltered. I questioned whether Indigenous people gave a shit what a white girl in buttfuck nowhere did for Thanksgiving. Maybe I *was* virtue signaling. Or maybe I just cared about my own feelings. Maybe I just didn't want to feel shitty for celebrating something awful. Maybe it was all about me. I worried I was trying to channel my distress about Greta into this. Maybe I felt guilty and took on caring about what she cared about to fill the gap she'd left. I wasn't qualified to fill that gap; I am not very well-read. I also knew that my take on this might be completely off. Greta used to talk incessantly about how ignorant she was, and I knew I was even more ignorant than her.

After a pregnant pause, I said, *"I'm sorry, Jerry. I can't come."*
She asked me why.
I inhaled and prepared to explain myself, but then her voice broke. She said, *"Why not?"* She said she had already made me

sweet-potato casserole. She told me, *"No one else eats that but you."* She told me Marg was coming. She was driving in from college. She knew Marg and I barely spoke anymore. She said, *"You'd just have to come from across town. It's like five minutes. What are you doing? Do you have other plans? You could just come for an hour. This is mean, Sigrid. It hurts my feelings. It means a lot to me that you come."*

While she ranted, I questioned myself. I wondered if maybe I was exploiting genocide to get out of spending Thanksgiving with my family. I didn't like going to family dinners anymore. Jerry was always trying to get us to ingest essential oils. It felt like my mom spent the entire time spewing constant flagrant pejoratives. I sat biting my inner cheeks, getting nudged by Margit whenever I opened my mouth.

My family is small. Most holiday dinners included my parents, Margit, and Jerry. Occasionally, when Jerry had a boyfriend, he came, and his kids if he had kids. Grandma used to be there too, but she died. I found her absence uncomfortable. It felt like someone was missing. On top of hating our dinner conversations, feeling on edge and judged, I felt bereft.

"I don't want to celebrate someone's day of mourning," I said quickly.

"What? What did you say?" she asked.

I inhaled, preparing to repeat myself, but I felt beaten down.

"Sorry," I said. *"Never mind. I'll come."*

———

Before we ate, I sat in the living room with Jerry's new boyfriend's son, Billy. The rest of the family were in the next room. They were playing cards, or backgammon, or something. We were sipping apple cider that tasted like it had rosemary oil in it, watching Jerry's Great Dane roll on the rug in front of us.

It was quiet. Occasionally Billy turned to ask me a question.

At one point, he asked me who I was texting. I wasn't texting anyone. I was rereading old messages from Greta.

He said, *"Come on. Who is it?"*

I said, *"No one."*

He repeated, *"Come on. Tell me."*

I said, *"Fine. Greta Gardener."*

He said, *"Oh, I know her. She dated a friend of mine."*

I frowned. *"What? Who?"*

As far as I knew, she had never had a girlfriend.

He replied, *"Kevin Fliner."*

I made a face. That was the creep who assaulted her at the party in high school.

"He's running for mayor," he continued, not noticing my reaction. *"He's got a great platform. He really cares about combating homelessness and strengthening our law enforcement."*

I didn't know how to reply. I was shaken to learn Kevin referred to Greta as his ex-girlfriend. That was a bizarre lie. It signaled that he remembered what happened. I assumed he'd forgotten; that he was drunk and made a mindless, vile mistake. But he hadn't forgotten if he was out in the world telling people they dated. He couldn't possibly believe that they had really dated, because they didn't. The only thing that ever happened between them was the night he assaulted her and the brief group breakfast the next morning. She barely knew him.

Billy kept talking. *"He's married. His wife is pregnant. Great dude. He's going to be the youngest mayor in Drysdale history."*

The dog started barking at the patio door, so I stood up. I slid the door open for her and stepped out into the darkness. I crossed my arms and exhaled while she squatted in the grass.

I returned to my apartment after Thanksgiving and stewed about Kevin. I also stewed about my family. At one point, before we ate dinner, we went around the table and said what we were thankful for. Jerry said something about essential oils. Dad said something about sports. When it was my turn, some misguided demon possessed me to say I was thankful for the resilience of Indigenous people. Everyone made faces at me as if I had said something batshit. Billy cracked some joke about me being a social justice warrior, and Margit nudged my ribs.

Later, while we were eating, my dad said, *"Sigrid, did you know everyone here is technically Indigenous because we were all born here?"*

My face got hot. I said, *"No, we're not, and that's an incredibly stupid thing to say,"* and he rolled his eyes at me as if I were the one being antagonistic.

"That's not stupid, it's true," my mom said.

Marg nudged my ribs again. I looked at Jerry. She was visibly drained from a full day of cooking. She kept rolling oils on her wrists. I held my tongue. I repressed my impulse to tell everyone to fuck off. I ate my mashed potatoes and squash rather than fling them at everyone. The room went on to discuss the election. Billy told everyone to vote for Kevin. He told them how much he cared about combating illegal drug use. I knew if I said anything, it would snowball. I'd end up screaming. My dad kept saying, *"Wow!"*

"He sounds fantastic!"

"We need a man like that!"

When I got home, I undressed in my bathroom and inspected the bruises Marg poked into my ribs. I cried while I ate the leftover sweet-potato casserole that Jerry sent home with me, while I wondered what stupid things I thought and did because I was raised in a cesspool of ignorance. I fell asleep reading Greta's old texts and worrying about my esophagus and my gut lining, knowing that Jerry probably infused all the Thanksgiving food with oils that humans aren't supposed to ingest.

Four

At Christmas I found myself next to Billy again. Everyone else was in the next room, playing cards, or some board game. We were sipping strawberry wine beside Jerry's Christmas tree. I gawked at the tinsel, wondering if it was intended to look like ice. Was it designed to? It was draping from the branches, mirroring the lights. In my mind, the tree looked frozen.

I looked away from it and glanced down at my hands. I thought about how it was a fake plastic tree, covered in fake plastic ice, masquerading as a wintry plant. Real trees smell like pine. They need water. They shed their needles and turn brown. Jerry's tree was pretend.

Billy brought up Kevin again. He said, *"So, your friend's ex-boyfriend's campaign is looking good. He's favored to win."*

Without giving it much thought, I corrected him. I said, *"He's not her ex-boyfriend."*

Billy said, *"Oh, he's not? He said he was—"*

I said, *"No. He sexually assaulted her at a party once, though. Maybe he thinks of that as dating."*

He choked on his wine.

I didn't mean to shock him. I was just feeling a little drunk and blunt. I had stewed about this since Thanksgiving and felt angry. It wasn't my business to share that information, but I did it anyway. I didn't want Billy to refer to Kevin as her ex-boyfriend again. I thought if I continued to nod along to that lie, I would have to live like it were true, and it wasn't. It bothered me.

His shock knocked me out of my tinsel trance.

He said, *"Are you being serious? When?"*

I told him it happened when she was seventeen.

He stammered. He asked if I was sure.

I nodded. *"Yes. Absolutely."*

He said, *"What did he do exactly? Did he just cop a feel? Was it like . . ."*

I frowned at him for saying "just cop a feel," as if that's tolerable. I tried to say what it was exactly, but I stumbled. I said, *"No, it was—it was . . ."*

"Rape?" he whispered.

I said, *"Yeah. He had sex with her without her permission while she told him she was gay."*

He gasped, *"She's gay?"*

That made me laugh. It broke the tension. I almost spit a mouthful of wine on the carpet. Billy laughed awkwardly with me, recognizing the preposterousness of zeroing in on Greta's gayness when that wasn't the focal point of the story. His face turned bright pink.

Marg entered the room around this time. She brought a platter of sugar cookies and marshmallow peanut butter squares. She asked, *"What's so funny?"*

Rather than reply, *Sigrid was just telling me about how her friend was raped and is a lesbian,* Billy said, *"Oh, we're just laughing at the dog."*

The dog was sitting in front of us. She looked at me in a way that made me feel like, somehow, she understood what we were talking about. I could sense that she didn't think highly of Billy.

We each ate one of the squares Marg brought and chatted with her about her classes. She was in a Renaissance Literature class that she liked. She told us about *Paradise Lost*.

Later that evening, she and I got into a fight because I lost my cool and threw pie guts at Mom. I watched Marg scold me, and realized she didn't understand my perspective. She wanted to maintain peace, ignore our problems, and placate everyone. Her objective was to avoid conflict. Mine wasn't. I wanted issues to be acknowledged. I wanted to address it when our family behaved badly. I was sick of playing along. I felt like I was a black sheep, and she was an enabler. I was the target of everyone's frustration, and she kept the peace for everyone but me. I remember standing outside, trying to leave, while Marg cried that I was upsetting everyone. She told me to grit my teeth more, like she did.

I felt like I was falling down a well, and rather than offer a hand, Margit reprimanded me for screaming. I wanted to unload on her. I wanted to scream that our family was voting for a rapist who assaulted my friend. I didn't get to escape to college, make new friends, or get any reprieve from Drysdale and our family, like she did. I had to stew there in a pot of Jerry's essential oils, while I watched my friend disintegrate. I felt all alone. It was intolerable to feel that way and be pelted by my family's ignorance. I was distraught by the fact that our family supported Kevin. It made me feel like all the light on earth had gone out.

When I was a kid, I loved being around my family. Listening to my mom, Grandma, and Jerry laugh felt comforting, like hearing birds chirp. I liked to eavesdrop on my dad talking to whoever Jerry was dating at the time. I would sit between them, with my face resting on my knuckles, thinking my dad was so smart. There was a comforting smell I associated with holidays and our family. It's this mix of cigarette smoke, potatoes, and gravy. I used to love existing in the chatter of our family, breathing in that familiar smell.

A veil was lifted when I got older. A lot of the glittery happiness brushed off when I understood more of what was being said around me. Dad was often making offhand racist comments. Everyone was always laughing at sexist jokes that weren't funny. I found myself huffing that smoky potato smell, trying to cling to the nostalgia of my childhood, while being pelted with intermittent homophobic remarks about feminine boys and women who don't shave their armpits.

I don't shave my armpits. I wear clothes that don't expose that around them. I wear high-collared shirts so they can't see my shark tattoo. I keep my socks on even when they are dirty, so they can't see the piece of Lego I have tattooed to my foot. I had to hide who I was around them. I felt disconnected from them. Like I was a stranger. I felt lonelier around them than I did when I was by myself.

Five

When I played with my toys in our basement, I listened to my family above me. I could identify who everyone was by the creak their steps made on the floor. I knew if the person walking was my mom, Dad, Margit, or our cat Lou by how heavily they stepped, and how fast they moved.

Dad was heavy-footed. He always moved furniture around. He dropped things a lot. He swung doors open like there was a surprise behind them.

My mom walked briskly, always in a rush. She slammed cupboards. She was often sweeping. I heard her kneel down to pick things up off the floor.

Margit walked lightly. She tiptoed. She turned doorknobs entirely before pushing doors open and shut them with the doorknob still cranked, so the door would fit back into its frame as quietly as possible. She never slammed the cupboards.

Lou, our cat, stepped unabashedly, with no consideration regarding whether she was making the floors creak. I could hear her paws stomp across the floor. When she came down the basement stairs, each of her steps thudded. She walked without questioning whether her steps could be lighter. She occupied the space she was in with the weight that she was.

I could gauge everyone's mood by the noises above me. I could sense when my parents were in bad moods—when they had transformed into swamp-monsters—by how fast they moved, and how hard they stepped. When they were angry, dust showered down from the beams in the ceiling. It rained on me and my toys. When that happened, I hid in the basement like a bird before a tsunami.

When I was little, I thought adults fought for serious, important reasons. I thought of their anger the way I thought of natural disasters. I considered it unavoidable—an unfortunate matter of fate.

When there were swamp-monsters stomping in my sky, I played that there was a storm in the basement. I played that the sound of breaking glass was thunder. When people shouted, it was heavy rain. The storm ended when it got quiet, the dust settled, and everyone walked quickly.

I didn't leave the basement until the house had been silent for hours. When I finally emerged, the main floor felt like a town after a volcanic eruption. Everything looked eerie and still.

Occasionally, I crawled halfway up the basement staircase when the fights were still in progress. I looked through the crack under the door at everyone's feet, like a mouse. Typically, Swamp-Monster Dad was screaming threats. Sometimes, he threw things. Once in a while, Swamp-Monster Mom got violent. Dad was much bigger than she was, though. It was a considerably worse storm when he was the one instigating thunder. Margit was always mute no matter what was happening. I rarely ever went further than halfway up the stairs.

When the arguments got really bad, Jerry brought us to her house. I think Margit snuck off and called her to come get us. I usually brought Jo with me. I pretended the toy world was planning Jo a surprise party, and that we had to leave the house so they could decorate.

In December, I read every article Greta ever sent me. At first I was reading them to connect with her when I couldn't anymore; however, I inadvertently learned a lot. Greta had referenced books sometimes in our conversations. I got a library card to read them. When the library didn't have copies, I filled out forms requesting that they buy them. I learned about interlibrary loans.

Largely because of what I was reading, I began caring about local government. I followed our election closely. I started to understand the impact it can have on the quality of people's lives. I read Kevin's platform.

If Kevin had never assaulted my friend, I'd still hate him. I think he's a harmful person regardless of what he did to Greta at that party; however, it's especially difficult to stomach my family supporting him when I know with absolute certainty that he is a bad person.

Despite trying to prove people wrong, I know that I'm an idiot. I have a history of bad judgment. I didn't graduate high school. I've climbed up the sides of crumbling silos at night. I've snorted Oxy-Contin off a butter knife in a stranger's garage. Despite my recent reading, and because of it, I know I am ignorant; however, the only thing I am more certain of than my own ignorance is Kevin's.

He said things like, "*Our city needs to spend less on rainbow flags and more on our police force.*" Or, "*We need to care about the people of Drysdale first; maybe there's room for refugees in Walkersville.*"

Whenever he mentioned anything about women, he mentioned that he had a wife and a mother—as if they were credentials and not human beings. He wanted to cut funding to the library and to disability support programs. He planned to combat the opioid epidemic by arresting homeless people and not letting them use the bus.

Jerry and my parents are going to vote for Kevin. My parents even have his lawn sign. I couldn't stand to be around them. I felt at odds with them. It made me worry they were bad people too.

Six

There are nice things about Drysdale. Main Street looks a lot like a Hallmark movie set. There's this giant bell at city hall that rings every hour. I always liked that sound. We're only forty minutes away from a bigger city, where everyone shops at the mall and goes off to college before returning here to plant their roots and picket fence stakes forever. When I was a kid, I liked picking blueberries at this old-world farm on the outskirts of town. I remember lying on the lawn in my parents' backyard, looking up at white clouds rolling through blue skies, believing I was in a good place on the planet.

I see things differently now. There are people in town who picket against painting a rainbow crosswalk. The newspaper prints comics seemingly set in the 1950s, where the husband hates his old ball and chain. There is a community Facebook page that might as well be a hate group. There is rarely hesitation before someone utters the

N-word or the F-slur. Confronting people feels like jumping into a fire. They hiss, *"How am I supposed to keep up with all these words?"*

I once made the mistake of informing my dad that he was cis, and he snapped, *"What the hell did you just call me?"*

I said, *"No, Dad. You're cisgendered. It just means—"*

He said, *"I am no such fucking thing!"*

I don't know what I was doing. I had this terrible compulsion to press my point. I couldn't stop myself from saying, *"Oh? Are you coming out, Dad?"*

He threw a hardcover book at me. The corner of it almost got me in the eye. I screamed that he was an idiot. He screamed that I was an idiot. We both stood, furious, red-faced idiots.

That's what it's like here. Small talk regularly includes complaining about the opioid problem as if the subjects of that are the scum of the earth. Even discussing the weather is unsafe. People say, *"How's this for global warming?"* when it's cold out. There has never been a lady mayor. Everyone in town is baffled when a pro-choice politician is federally elected because they don't know a single person who voted for them. They think it has all been rigged. For some reason, asking for no meat in your salad invites strangers to scoff at you. I've had to lie to restaurants and say, "I'm not a vegetarian. I'm just on a diet," or risk verbal assault. I was afraid to hold a girl's hand or to appear as anything but their friend outside of my dark, musty basement. In the sparse times when I found anyone to date, we lived like vampires who surfaced from the ground at night.

I'm not interested in making small talk with people who offend or insult me. I want to admit to being a vegetarian in restaurants. I want to go outside in the daytime.

Seven

I googled Kevin. Most of his social media was private. I could see his friend list and a few photos. There was one picture of him in a suit holding both his thumbs up next to his political lawn sign. He had a wedding photo captioned, LOVE IS A MANY SPLENDORED THING. Among his friend list, I saw a few acquaintances of mine—including Billy.

While looking through his friend list, I noticed he was connected with a girl I once got into a fight with named Donna. Donna liked a lot of Kevin's photos. She also commented beneath them enough to suggest they were good friends.

I clicked on her profile. Her profile picture was of her as a little girl in her mother's lap. It was captioned, RIP MOM. I LOVE YOU. I liked the picture and thought, *Oh man, that's sad.* I then scrolled down into her profile.

Beneath the content about her mom, I discovered that Donna

posted incessantly about opposing gay marriage, not welcoming refugees, poor people exploiting "government handouts," drag queens being predators, the importance of conversion therapy, and about her conviction that both sexism and racism affected white men more than anyone. All of her likes were for bakeries that refused to make wedding cakes for gay couples and for plantation wedding venues. She had recently posted a photo of a rainbow and captioned it, RAINBOWS ARE A COVENANT FROM GOD, THEY ARE NOT GAY.

I grimaced. Donna devoted a worrying amount of time to posting hateful content. She wrote long blocks of text defending herself and got into debates in the comments. It was clear from her tone, and by the amount of content that she shared, this was a pastime of hers. It was like a hobby. It entertained her. It seemed like she was posting about reality TV and debating which contestant the bachelor should marry, and not like she was posting about other humans' safety and well-being.

After scouring her profile, I realized what bothered me most were her pictures of her mom. Right before posting that she died, there was a link to a petition barring trans people from the local farmer's market bathrooms. The posts about her mom made me angry because they exposed that Donna was able to turn everything else off. She could deprioritize her usual content when something bad happened to her.

I got fired up. I wrote on her wall:

> **Did you know that when you're a marginalized person, you can't just turn it off? You have to deal with people opposing your use of public washrooms even when your mom dies.**

After I typed that out, I considered erasing it. I often wrote out texts to my family that I never sent. After visiting them, I wrote long rants in my diary. I considered ripping those rants out and mailing them to everyone. Every time I looked at Jerry's Facebook, I resisted commenting. I internalized my disquiet until it manifested into this horrible, secret rage. In this case I surprised myself. I clicked post.

I was at the end of my rope. I had lost what little care I had when it came to speaking my mind. I felt devastated about Greta, incensed by Kevin, Donna, and people like them. I had nothing to lose.

Almost immediately, a stranger replied,

what the fuck? give donna a break right now.

Shortly after that, Donna replied,

wow. this is insane. how dare you? now is not the time.

I doubled down.

no. fuck you, donna.

Later that night, I dreamed that Donna was a doll in my basement. I pictured myself holding her, having her voice. If she were my toy, I would play that her storyline involved her seeing the light, making amends, and devoting herself to helping other people.

I fell asleep and dreamed in Donna's voice. I said, *I am so sorry, everyone. I have been awful, and I am going to change—*

But then little plastic Donna bit my finger.

I jumped. *Ouch. What the fuck?*

She shouted, *Don't put words in my mouth!*

I said, *What? Don't you want to be a good toy?*

She said, *I am a good toy.*

I said, *No you're not. You're a villain.*

She said, *No I'm not. You are.*
Then I woke up.

———————

I wish I could have existed in a bubble where snow really was icing, clouds were made of cotton candy, and everyone lived like rodents eating hot dogs. I think that could be possible. If everyone could just be rat-like, find a hot dog, and work together to turn rain into sugar.

It is strange what some people devote themselves to. When I think of the moments that I was glad to be alive, everyone was happy. I don't relish a single second I was around anyone who felt miserable. Any time I had to face something sad, I did so out of obligation. I would never, for example, slow down by a car accident or a house fire to appreciate the wreckage. I would prefer to speed by with my eyes closed tight, humming.

It's strange to me that people like Donna are so drawn to misery. I don't like misery. I think that's partially why I hated *Hamlet*. If I could choose, my entire life story wouldn't have had any conflict. No one would ever get sick. No one would argue. We would all live happily forever.

I remember reading fairy tales when I was a kid and focusing less on the wolves in old lady clothing than I did on the cottages made of gingerbread. I remember thinking the world was going to have more talking mice and fairy godmothers, and less witches poisoning apples, or wolves eating naïve girls.

———————

I don't think the big bad wolf could eat me today. I'd be able to tell he was a wolf in grandma drag, and he'd be able to tell I wasn't a naïve girl. I'm too big to eat. I'm not a kid.

I can't retreat to the basement and pretend my parents' arguments are just thunder. I can't act like things are different than they are. I have to face the reality I live in. I am a grown-up now.

I had a Ken doll when I was a kid. My mom bought him for me at a yard sale for like a nickel. He wasn't a real Ken doll. He was off-brand. His arms weren't proportionate, and he didn't have ears. I didn't like the look of him.

I always played that the toys in my basement were happy. They had parties, sleepovers, and went swimming in the garbage can pools I made for them.

When I got Ken, Margit came down to the basement. She wanted to play with him. She suggested we make him the bad guy. She said he could be the town villain. In an attempt to be a good sport, I tried to play along. Together, we played that Ken killed Jo's father, married her mother, and lived in her old mansion on a hill near the water heater. We played that Jo had to move into a stable down the road and lived in poverty because of him.

I held Jo while we played this, but after a while I picked Ken up. I wanted to try playing the bad guy; however, I found it hard to speak in his voice. When I held him, I stopped making him bad. I started to explain away his behavior. I started playing that he didn't really kill Jo's dad. It was all a misunderstanding. He was a good toy too.

I used to think everyone was good. I knew we all had flaws, we made mistakes, and that some of those mistakes were awful, but at the end of the day—I believed we were all good guys. I thought that when people watched Disney movies, they never identified with the villains. Greta taught me the villains tended to be queer coded, and I did identify in some ways with Cruella and Ursula, but I never saw

myself as a bad guy. I was Simba; I wasn't Scar. I thought everyone
felt that way.

I started to think a lot about Kevin. He had campaign signs all over
town. I felt set off by his name. I thought of Greta and her life, and
him and his. I felt a lot of anger.

I tried to control that by thinking of everyone I knew and their
worst moments. I thought of my dad hitting my mom or throwing
a book at me. I thought of Jerry's Facebook posts, and of my mom
using the R-word. I thought of myself throwing pie, thrusting my
friend into an opioid addiction. I knew my hands weren't clean.

I always believed everyone was ultimately good. We were just
born in the world we were in; we were shaped in ways we wouldn't
have chosen to be had the world been created by us.

I wondered if it would be unfair to judge Kevin based on
one event that might not have truly represented him. I knew his
campaign was bad regardless of whether he was a rapist, but still. I
wondered if I were holding a Kevin doll, if he were the main character in my basement, would I really think he was bad?

I worried I would. Accepting that someone could be bad affected
my perception of reality. It felt similar to how I did when I realized I
didn't believe in God, or when I realized I was gay. The foundations
of all my beliefs were built on something false. If I accepted that
people could be bad, that would mean *I* could be.

I wondered, if I were a Barbie, would I pick myself up?

I imagined myself as a doll. I pictured that my skin was that soft
PVC plastic, and that my hard, jointless wrists were cuffed in twist
ties. I pictured spotting myself on a shelf in Walmart, inside a pink
cardboard box, behind a sheet of transparent plastic.

I decided that if I were a doll, I wouldn't have picked myself
up. That was when I decided to kill myself. I didn't like myself.

When I was a kid, I thought I would grow up to be someone different. I thought I'd be a better person, with a better life, in a better world.

I can't explain why I tried to kill myself. I'm embarrassed writing about it now. As I'm sure you can imagine, I wasn't in a good headspace. I made a rash choice when I felt particularly out of sorts.

I think part of why losing Greta feels so catastrophic is because she was the only person who I felt understood me, and who I understood. I felt alone without her.

I get this desperate feeling sometimes. Like I'm a kid banging inside the cage of my adult body, dying to escape to the moon. I get this terrible sense that I'm trapped all alone. I can't stand feeling like that. When I do, I'm frantic to escape; I can't think straight.

I really want to be happy.

Eight

When I woke up and realized my attempt failed, I panicked. I asked where my phone was. I begged a nurse to help me find it.

He couldn't. No one could. Everyone assured me it was fine, it didn't matter where my phone was, but I repeated that I needed it. I cried.

My phone showed that I had made calls I didn't want people to know about.

After several exchanges involving me pleading with hospital staff for my phone, I started to worry that I was being taken for a ride. I wondered if the nurses weren't telling me where my phone was because they'd confiscated it. Maybe they didn't want to tell me its whereabouts because I was in a delicate state, and they knew it would rattle me.

When Marg called my hospital room, I asked her if she had my phone. The way she answered was strange. She said she couldn't remember.

I called the Dollar Pal from a hospital phone. I expected to be dead, and I hadn't given them proper notice. After coming to terms with being alive, I realized they must be wondering where I disappeared to. I rang the store, but my manager told me Marg had already called. She told him I had an unforeseen medical emergency, and that I would be away. He asked how I was doing and said he was thinking of me.

I was surprised to learn Marg thought to call the store. I shouldn't have been. In retrospect, I should have known Marg would be on top of that. She thinks too much.

He asked what happened. I guess she didn't give him specifics.

"I'm not sure," I lied. "I was in an accident. I was comatose until today."

I tried to change the subject. I asked how the store was doing.

He said, "Oh wow, I'm glad you're okay. The store is fine. The usual. Well, we had another bomb threat yesterday. The cops are getting angry. Did you hear it was on the news?"

Marg called me after that phone call.

I asked her again, "Do you have my phone?"

She repeated, "I don't remember."

I have a good memory. Sometimes I get a whiff of this plant in the spring that reminds me of being a kid. I'm not sure what it is. It has a strong scent. It smells like vanilla and honey. It's a native plant, I think. It grows wild everywhere. Whenever I smell it, I feel like I'm inhaling my childhood. I almost believe that when I open my eyes, I'll be a kid outside in Drysdale again. I'll have Band-Aids stuck to my knees and wobbly baby teeth.

Marg was a handful when she was little. I think it's because she was smart. She was anxious with strangers, and she cried a lot. My parents told me they were worried when they found out Mom was pregnant with me. They thought it would be a nightmare having two babies so close in age. They figured I'd be just like Marg.

I wasn't like Marg after all.

One night, a few months ago, I walked through the cemetery uptown and thought about growing up. I decided that deep down we're all who we were when we were kids. I think being a teenager is about hiding all your quirks and contorting yourself to fit in and impress people, and being an adult is about re-finding who you were when you were eight years old.

I felt like I had to become someone new to grow up. I changed a lot. I became more jaded and serious. I was happier when I was a kid. I was more creative, and I cared less about what other people thought of me. I wish I could go back in time, reconnect with my genuine interests, let go of all social expectations, and feel happy as myself.

The problem is my child-self wouldn't operate well in the world. Serious people, who do what's expected of them, live easier lives. It's hard for me to reconcile being my authentic self with existing comfortably.

I think I was born to be happy. I was given a nature better suited for someone who could live lightheartedly. I feel like I'm a happy person, caged. I feel like I have the soul of some sunny kid, but it's been entombed in this awful swamp-monster body.

Before my suicide attempt, I felt rows of teeth split through my gums. I saw my skin turning green. I wanted to thrash in bog water. I had this insatiable desire to propel myself into a bayou, and to swallow a school of fish whole.

I don't want to be a swamp-monster. I don't want to be someone who hurts people. I don't think I was meant to be that. I think I was meant to be a rat.

I felt hopeless thinking of Kevin becoming mayor, and Greta overdosing, while I stood stranded at a cash register, wondering who was pocketing all the googly eyes. I felt myself getting older, sadder, and angrier.

You know how kids play with those plastic fruits and kitchen sets? I think they're practicing. One day, all their plastic bananas and oranges will become real fruits that can be eaten or can rot. The kitchen sinks will stop being Fisher-Price, and none of it will be a game anymore. Kids who play house and rock dolls in their arms will cradle real, living babies when they're grown-ups. Pretend cars will become actual machines that they have to make monthly payments on.

In a recent therapy session, I told Dr. Jeong a theory. I said I thought that maybe losing Jo was practice for losing Greta. Maybe I lost my doll to train my heart for losing my best friend. I told her that after I lost Jo, I packed all my toys up and ended my little world in the basement. I said, looking back, I think I could have handled things differently. I could have kept playing. I would have had to acknowledge that Jo was lost, though, and I didn't like the idea of playing like that.

Dr. Jeong suggested I could think about it differently. She suggested I could choose to believe that the raccoon breaking in was practice for Greta. I could hope that other people will help me clean and prop my fences and trees back up. That somehow, with some help, Greta will be pulled back.

If anyone had told me that a month ago, I would have rolled my eyes.

If I could pick how the world worked, Greta would kick her habit. I'd find her in the woods, sitting on a tree stump, combing mud out of Jo's hair. Kevin would be run out of town by a pitchfork-wielding mob, then he'd repent and change. The city would paint every crosswalk rainbow. Everyone would understand everyone, and we would all sincerely care about each other. No one would ever think about hurting people or killing themselves. The clouds would all turn pink.

Margit got rid of my phone and my journal. She destroyed everything incriminating in my apartment. She said she was forging my suicide note to console people, and to make sense of what happened, but that wasn't the whole truth. She also wrote it to hide something.

She pretended I was dating someone, but I wasn't. She made a girl up. She was trying to make my family, the cops, or anyone reading believe that some anonymous girl—someone who didn't even know my name—was traipsing around Drysdale with me. She wrote that she was lawless and reckless, that she keyed cop cars, and suspiciously showed up to pick me up every time there was a bomb threat. She wrote that so anyone reading would suspect her, so I wouldn't be blamed.

The truth is, I didn't spend the time before my attempt pool hopping or eating caviar. I spent it alone. I walked from work to my apartment. I stood in the Dollar Pal, scanning canned beans and toilet brushes, watching the clock tick until I could go home and lie in my bed. I spent my time alone rereading old emails and texts from Greta, following the local election, and stewing about how much I resented my family, Drysdale, and the universe. I wrote long diary entries about how much I hated it here, and how helpless I felt.

I made the bomb threats. Well, I made most of them. I didn't make the one that happened while I was unconscious in the hospital. Margit made that one to negate any suspicion that it was me.

I liked seeing Kevin evacuate his office. I also wanted to escape the Dollar Pal. I wanted to stand outside, inhale fresh air, and observe Kevin squirm. He had to stand near me, across the street from the plaza. Sometimes he looked scared. He said things like, *"Who keeps doing this?"* and *"Do you think we're actually in danger?"* Other times he complained about how it wasted his time, and how disruptive it was. I liked feeling like I had control over something. I could make Kevin leave his office. I could disturb his day. I could scare him.

Before I tried to kill myself, I looked up how to make a pipe bomb. I was eyeing short sections of steel pipes and matches. I often daydreamed about actually bombing Kevin's office.

When I was younger, I would have never savored the thought of someone dying, but I started to think a lot about Kevin dying. I felt a rush, picturing it. I dreamed that he died more than once. I woke up disappointed that he was alive. I thought of him dying the way people think about their crushes; it was on my mind before I went to sleep, and when I woke up.

I don't know what I'm supposed to do. I don't want to stand under fluorescent lights for ten hours every day and watch the world rot. I want to see magic monster fingers in tree branches, and ride in cars with my head out the window like a dog. I wish I could move away. I wish everything were different. I don't want Greta to die, or live some miserable life, or for shitty people to be put in positions of power by my family. I want the sky to turn pink.

I don't think good people daydream about other people dying.

I don't think good people google how to make pipe bombs. Sometimes I think I should have played along more when Margit pretended there were bad guys. Maybe if I had practiced being a villain as a kid, I might be able to handle it now. I don't feel equipped to be a grown-up or a bad person. I don't want to be. I'm afraid that maybe the problem isn't just Kevin. It's me too.

I want to be a garden gnome. I want to live in a hollowed-out mushroom. I can't do that, sadly. I have to exist where I am, in the world I'm in. I think my options are to blow myself up, blow everything else up, or just endure it. I couldn't successfully blow myself up, I don't actually want to blow everything else up, and I don't know how to endure it.

I have to do something else.

Marg called me. She said, "Hey, I was just thinking of you. I saw a rat in a dumpster."

I breathed air out my nose. "That made you think of me?"

She said, "Yes. You remind me of vermin. Did you know they step from their toes to their heels, like you do?"

I frowned. "I don't do that."

She laughed. "Do you ever think about how humans are always testing on rats?"

I replied, "No. I never think of that."

She said, "Well, we've got all this research about how rats behave because we experiment on them so much. My roommate Candace was telling me about this. She's a psychology major. It's really interesting. She said rats help each other. They remember individual rats who helped them. Isn't that cool? They demonstrate empathy and avoid harming other rats."

I frowned. "I'm pretty sure some rats eat each other."

I looked at my hands and imagined I had little rat fingers. I imagined that Marg and I grew up in a rat's nest; that we were two little pink baby rats together.

"I'm sorry," I said.

"For what?" she asked.

"Just in general."

She didn't say anything.

"Did you know Jerry didn't vote for Kevin?" she asked.

Kevin won the election, like we expected.

I said, "She didn't? Are you sure?"

I was positive she did.

"Yeah, she told me she didn't because of you. She said you had a good talk."

I did talk to Jerry about Kevin, but I didn't think it was a good talk. In fact, I'd call it an argument. We raised our voices. I felt angry. I didn't think she was listening.

After some silence, I asked, "Remember when we packed up the basement?"

After I lost Jo, Marg helped me pack up my toys. She didn't ask me why I was packing. She just found me in the basement disassembling my dollhouses and started helping me. She wrapped my more delicate toys in old cloths before placing them in Rubbermaid bins. After everything was packed, we surveyed the bare concrete floor, and she said, *"You can always take them back out if you want to."*

She replied, "Yeah, I remember that."

I said, "Thanks for helping me."

She was quiet. She knew I didn't just mean about the basement. "You're welcome."

After a moment, she added, "We still have everything, you know. It's all still in the basement in boxes."

"Yeah. Maybe I should go through that sometime," I said.

"We could put everything back together. That might be fun. Or donate it, maybe. Or should we save it for our future kids if we have them?"

I nodded. "Maybe, yeah."

I thought about myself as a kid sitting on the ground in the basement, surrounded by dolls and toy animals. I thought of how Barbie doll hair smells, and the musty scent that's still in the basement today.

I said, "You know, when we were kids, I wanted to grow up, and for the world to be like our basement. I wanted the streets to be built to accommodate unicorns. You know what I mean? I wanted the clouds to look like the basement's insulation. But when I got older, I looked around and realized the clouds are usually white. Sometimes they're gray."

I was closing my eyes when I said this.

She said, "Have you been outside today?"

I was lying in my bed with the curtains closed. I said no.

She said, "Go outside. It rained earlier. The light is weird."

I sighed, climbed out of my bed, and ambled down the hall. I walked outside and stood on the asphalt driveway with no shoes on. The ground was wet, and I was moving cautiously, afraid I might step on a pebble or on some crushed glass. Broken bottles seem to materialize whenever I'm barefooted. I exhaled, looked up from my exposed feet, and saw the clouds above me were pink.

Acknowledgments

Thanks to my friends and family, especially Torren and Lou. I'm enormously grateful to my literary agent, Heather Carr. Thank you so much for all your work and support, Heather. Thank you also to Jade Hui, who thoughtfully edited and improved this book. I'm indebted to you, Jade.

I am grateful to everyone at Atria and Simon & Schuster Canada. Thanks especially to Gena Lanzi, Jolena Podolsky, Brittany Lavery, Cayley Pimentel, Kaycee Chapman, Stacey Sakal, and Kelli McAdams. Thanks also to everyone who has supported any of my writing, including everyone at the Friedrich Agency, the Canada Council for the Arts, the folks at Atlantic Books, my English teachers, booksellers, librarians, other writers, reviewers, bookish social media folks, and many others.

Thank you to Sigrid Forberg, who blindly let me use her name for this book with no idea what the character would be like.

I wrote this while listening to the songs "Devil Town" by Daniel Johnston, "Afraid of Heights" by boygenius, Noah Kahan's *Stick Season* album, and "Another Sun" by Tracy Chapman.

To anyone who has spent their time reading this, or anything I've written, I am really grateful.

About the Author

Emily Austin is the author of *Everyone in This Room Will Someday Be Dead, Interesting Facts about Space,* and the poetry collection *Gay Girl Prayers*. She was born in Ontario, Canada, and received two writing grants from the Canadian Council for the Arts. She studied English literature and library science at Western University. She currently lives in Ottawa, in the territory of the Anishinaabe Algonquin Nation.